TEDDY
ALMOST A WORLD RECORD BREAKER
MARS

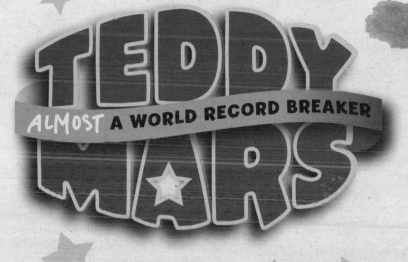

TEDDY MARS

ALMOST A WORLD RECORD BREAKER

MOLLY B. BURNHAM

Illustrations by
TREVOR SPENCER

SCHOLASTIC INC.

ISBN 978-0-545-90856-6

Text copyright © 2015 by Molly B. Burnham.
Illustrations copyright © 2015 by Trevor Spencer. All rights reserved.
Published by Scholastic Inc., 557 Broadway, New York, NY 10012,
by arrangement with Katherine Tegen Books, an imprint of
HarperCollins Children's Books, a division of HarperCollins Publishers.
SCHOLASTIC and associated logos are trademarks and/or registered
trademarks of Scholastic Inc.

12 11 10 9 8 7 6 5 4 3 2 1   15 16 17 18 19 20/0

Printed in the U.S.A.   40

First Scholastic printing, October 2015

Typography by Carla Weise

To my kids, Adelaide and Georgia.
You are my Exuberators, Choaticators,
and Hilariators.
In other words, my Inspirators.

MY BROTHER, JAKE

The day my brother climbed into the cat box was the day I knew my life would never be normal again.

And that's saying something because my life was not normal to begin with.

But Jake, he's like the first time you open *The Guinness Book of World Records*. All you can do is think about it all day long, even when your teacher hollers, "Teddy, it's the third day of school. Can you please save daydreaming until day four?"

"Strange but true, Ms. Raffeli, I'm not daydreaming. I'm thinking about fingernails and you'll be happy to know it's related to the math unit we're working on." I take her silence as a chance to explain.

"You know Lee Redmond, the lady with the longest fingernails?" She looks blank so I try to help her out. "From *The Guinness Book of World Records?*" She still looks blank. Was this lady ever a kid?

"Ms. Raffeli, you must know *The Guinness Book of World Records.* Even my parents know *The Guinness Book of World Records.*"

"Yes, Teddy, I know *The Guinness Book of World Records.*"

Phew! "So all ten of Lee Redmond's nails add up to 28 feet 4.5 inches, which is long. It's got to be longer than our class rug, and maybe taller than our walls."

Before Ms. Raffeli can respond, the new girl, Viva, pops up and says, "Let's measure it!" She grabs a measuring tape we've been using and starts measuring the rug, and then a bunch of other kids start measuring 28 feet 4.5 inches all over the room.

It turns out Lee Redmond's nails are shorter than the distance from the sink to the door, longer than twelve desks in a row, and twice as long as the rug.

Ms. Raffeli looks straight at me, eyebrows raised as tall as the tallest roller coaster (418 feet), and says, "You'd think after having five of the Mars kids, they'd give me a break. There are two other fourth grade teachers."

She's right of course; she's earned a break from my family. But for some reason no one else thinks so. Which means, just like my five sisters before me, Ms. Raffeli and I are stuck with each other for the year. At least she knows *The Guinness Book of World Records*.

But going back to my original point: the stuff you see in that book does not get out of your head.

28 feet
4.5 in

It's the same with Jake. Once you see your little brother curled up in a cat box, it's hard to picture him any other way.

LONNIE

Lonnie is my best friend and is the smartest person I know. He wants to be a Jedi when he grows up. Clearly, he's smart enough to know they don't really exist, but he wants to be something *like* a Jedi.

We've known each other since the first day of kindergarten, when we pulled out matching Star Wars action figures. Mr. Munz told us no toys at school. But Lonnie was smart even when we were five. He said, "Meet me at the art table. There aren't any rules about drawing." He was right, of course.

For the rest of the year, we drew Wookiees, droids, Jedi Masters with lightsabers, and Star Wars stuff we made up, and Mr. Munz never said a word.

Lonnie's mom still has all his old pictures. That's why I can remember them so well. My mom says that with seven kids she can't keep every picture we make. There aren't enough walls in the house.

RECORD ATTEMPTS 1, 2, AND 3

Lonnie and I love Star Wars. There's no replacing that, but this summer when I found *The Guinness Book of World Records* behind the sofa—well, I got seriously hooked.

Of course, it's an old copy. My family doesn't buy anything new. No one knows how it got there. Grace tried to say it was hers but my mom didn't go along with her this time, so I got to keep it. And I don't care how old the book is, it's awesome!

Ever since then I've been trying to break a world record of my own. So far it has not been successful. Stuffing the most grapes in my mouth seemed good but I only got to ten before my cheeks hurt so much that I spit them out. Clearly, ten grapes won't cut it.

I thought I was on a roll with the most jumping jacks but after twenty minutes I got a stomach cramp.

And even though I seriously thought skateboarding down my banister would be cool, it seemed dumb once I was up there. The banister isn't that long so I was pretty sure it wouldn't actually get me into *The Guinness Book of World Records* and probably all it would do is break something.

And now, Ms. Raffeli says I can't bring the book to school anymore.

"Too distracting," she says.

"I admit," I say, "when I found Garry Turner, the guy with the most clothespins clipped on his face"—159!!!!—"I was distracted."

"The book stays home," she says. "And that's final."

VIVA'S MIND TRICK

Lonnie and I sit at our regular table in the lunchroom. We've been here since first grade when we got to pick our seats. It's the table in the corner, closest to the trash cans. We like to sit alone, and because of the trash cans no one else likes to sit with us.

Until this year.

This year Viva started at our school. She's the one who created the measuring debacle today, which somehow I got blamed for. On top of that, she's decided to sit at our table. She just sits here. I don't know why. There are plenty of seats all over the place, but she sits here. So far she doesn't talk to us. Just eats. So long as it stays like that I guess it doesn't matter.

"Lonnie, you won't believe this," I say as I bite into my sandwich. The bread is a little stale. "Jake got lost yesterday."

"You lost Jake?" he says. "Again?"

"Who's Jake?" Viva is leaning across the table, her sandwich frozen in midair, the only thing in

the whole room that is not moving.

Before I can stop Lonnie, he says, "Teddy's little brother."

"Oh great," I mutter to Lonnie. "This is exactly what I do not want." I look at Viva. "It's nothing."

"Come on," she says. "Losing a brother is something."

"It's really nothing," I say again.

"I think it's something," she says.

"There's no use, Teddy," Lonnie whispers. "You can't fight her. She's like Yoda. She's got powers."

Viva may be new to our school, but Lonnie has her figured out. It's part of his Jedi training.

I chew my sandwich. Viva stares at me and I'd swear she's using the Jedi Mind Trick except her hand isn't waving around.

MORE ABOUT THE CAT BOX

"Okay, okay," I say. "Quit eyeballing me." I look at Lonnie, and only Lonnie. "So like I was saying, Jake disappeared—"

"How old is Jake?" Viva asks.

I roll my eyes. "Four." Explaining every detail of this story to a complete stranger is not what I planned or wanted, but somehow I am. Lonnie's got to be right, it's the Yoda in her.

"Were your parents worried?" she asks.

"No, we knew he was somewhere in the house."

Lonnie slurps his milk and says, "They have seven kids. They're not like normal parents."

"Seven?!"

I'm used to this response but I still turn red.

"Go on," Lonnie says.

"We looked in all his usual hideouts—"

Viva interrupts, "His usual hideouts?"

Lonnie explains, "Like the cabinets, under the bed, in his closet, places like that."

I ignore Viva's look of confusion. "He was nowhere. But I went back into the kitchen because I had a feeling he was there—even though we'd already looked. That's when I noticed Smarty Pants—"

"Who's Smarty Pants?" Viva asks.

"Our cat," I say. "She was standing just outside her cat box."

"What's a cat box?" Viva asks.

"A cat's toilet," I say.

"You mean litter box."

"No, I mean cat box. That's what we call it."

"Is it the covered kind?"

"Yes," I say. "Can I please finish?"

"Go ahead," she says and bites her sandwich like I'm the one who's interrupting her.

"So there's Smarty Pants meowing at it. I was the only one in the kitchen, so I looked."

"In the litter box?" she asks.

"In the cat box," I say. "And there he was. Curled up like a bird in a nest, snoring."

"Except birds can't snore," Lonnie says.

Viva's eyes are big. "How did he fit?"

"He's a contortionist," Lonnie explains. "He's always liked small places. And he's small for his age."

"So what did you do?"

"Called to my mom."

"What did your mom do?"

"She said, 'It's a good thing I cleaned that out this morning, or Jake would be covered in poo.'"

Lonnie laughs. "Your mom is the best."

"Then what?" Viva asks.

"She pulled him out." I take a bite of my sandwich.

"Do you have to eat meals with this brother of yours? It seems kind of gross."

"Actually, Jake eats in the cabinet with the pots and pans."

"Your parents let your little brother eat in a cabinet?" The recess bell rings and we stand up, except for Viva, who looks at me and says, "Your family is different. Very different."

MY DIFFERENT FAMILY

1. **Sharon, the singer** (seventeen): Give her a dirty, stinky sock and she'll make up a song about it and sing it everywhere. For months. Of course, she'd never take a dirty, stinky sock from anyone.

2 and 3. **Caitlin and Casey, the twins** (fourteen): They are always together, and no one except us can tell them apart.

4. **Maggie, the runner** (thirteen): Doesn't care

which sport she plays, so long as she can run, run, run. But she really likes soccer the most.

5. **Grace, the lemon** (twelve): With a name like Grace you'd think she'd be nice. She isn't. She's like a lemon except at least with lemons you can always add sugar. There isn't enough sugar in the world to make Grace sweet. I'm seriously not joking.

6. **Me, the boy** (nine and eleven-twelfths): I'll be ten in three weeks. My birthday is October 2.
7. **Jake, the other boy:** He's been around for four miserable years. My parents call him the surprise. I call him a pain. The kind I would have if I got in *The Guinness Book of World Records* for lifting 113 pounds 15 ounces with my ear. That has got to be a pain. Not as much as my brother, but still a pain.

★ MY BIRTHDAY LIST ★

1. A new tent. You remember what Jake did to the old one. (Right?)

MY FAMILY IS LIKE A TONGUE

Living in a big family is not easy. Being Stephen Taylor must not be easy either. He's the man with the longest tongue (3.86 inches). *The Guinness Book of World Records* only measures the part that sticks out past your lips, so it might not sound long, but I measured my tongue and it only sticks out 1.3 inches. So you see, 3.86 inches is LONG.

Strange but true, there are similarities between a large family and a large tongue.

1. You know a large tongue must get in the way. I can honestly say that five sisters and a little brother get in my way.
2. The gross factor: a tongue is gross, a huge tongue is grosser, a huge family is the grossest. There is no privacy. I've seen things I would not repeat for all the soda in the world. Sure, if we were rich and lived in a mansion it would be different. But try to find a little space of your own. A place no one else is, has been, or will be. It won't happen unless you're Jake and a cat box doesn't make you want to puke. Really I might as well search for the Planck Length, which according to *The Guinness Book of World Records* is the smallest unit of length in the universe. If the length were measured in centimeters, it would have a decimal point, then thirty-four zeroes, and then finally the number one, like this: 0.00000000000000000000 0000000000000001. What I'm trying to say is: I'm never going to find the Planck Length and I'm never going to find a place of my own.
3. I don't actually have a third point but Ms.

Raffeli says we're supposed to think of three points to make in our essays, and she's a serious lady. So I'll have to think of a third one.

GRUMPY PIGEON MAN

A lot of days when I get home from school, I sneak into my backyard. If you knew Mr. Marney, our next-door neighbor, you'd sneak too.

I call him Grumpy Pigeon Man (never to his face) because he's grumpy and he keeps pigeons. Not that I know anything about those pigeons, because the guy doesn't talk; he grunts, groans, and grumbles, pretty much about the noise my family makes and the trees in our backyard that drop leaves everywhere. The guy hates leaves.

A chain-link fence separates our yards, which means there's not much privacy, which means he can gripe as much as he wants, but it also means I can see his pigeons.

Anyway, the pigeons have a special house of their own in his backyard and every day Grumpy Pigeon Man lets them fly around free. I mean free up in the sky. They never scatter or fly away. They fly in a big circle. And then they always come home. Just like a boomerang.

The pigeons are why I sneak outside. Watching them fly around is cool. Getting caught by Grumpy Pigeon Man is not, which is why I'm running back into my house right now.

Anyway, I'd rather deal with anything more than Grumpy Pigeon Man. Actually it's a tie between him and Jake.

I still can't decide who is worse.

★ MY BIRTHDAY LIST #2 ★

1. A new tent because Jake destroyed the old one last summer. (You do remember that, don't you?)

2. A book about pigeons.

TWO CAT BOXES

Mom bought another. Really. Another cat box just for Jake.

"We decided Jake should have his own," she explains over dinner. "He likes it so much, but it was Smarty Pants's. It didn't seem right for him to take over her cat box. And I just can't clean it that often." She leans down and gives more potatoes to Jake, who's eating dinner under the table in his new cat box.

"And it's portable," Dad adds. "We can move him around." He actually sounds happy about this.

"Is he going to eat in there every night?" Sharon asks. She practically sings this because she practically sings everything. "If he gets to do that I want to eat in my room."

"If Sharon gets to eat in her room, then we want to eat in our room," Caitlin and Casey say together. No matter how often they do it, it's still weird when they talk at the same time.

"I don't care where I eat," Maggie says, scooping up her last bite. "I'm going for a run."

Grace stomps on my foot for no reason at all. "Ouch!" I say.

"Sorry," she says. But she's not.

Mom silences us. "You will all stay where you

are until we finish dinner. And no," she says to Sharon, "you will not eat in your room. After the six of you, I've seen everything, and one of these days Jake will eat with the rest of us."

"I am eating with you," Jake says from his cat box.

Mom bends down. "I mean at the table, hon." Then she pops back up and says, "I don't want to hear another word about it."

PECULIAR RUNS IN THE FAMILY

A few days after moving into the cat box, Jake decides to eat only yellow foods.

"Jake," Mom says, "cereal is yellow."

"It's not yellow."

"The cereal is yellow."

"Mom, the cereal is not yellow. It's gray. And the milk is white."

"I can make it yellow."

"Mom," Grace says. "That's gross. I don't think Jake should eat yellow snow or yellow milk."

"Grace, it's food coloring."

"I cannot believe this," I say. "You're going to dye his food a different color so he'll eat it? What happened to 'eat what's on your plate'?"

"Teddy, that has never happened in this household. As I recall you went through a phase of eating only orange foods. Carrots, carrot cake, pumpkin, pumpkin pie, oranges."

"I don't remember that."

Grace snorts but Mom stops her. "Don't start. When you were three you would only wear black. Even your undies had to be dyed black. They don't make black underwear for three-year-olds."

Clearly, peculiar just runs in my family.

RECORD ATTEMPT 4

Georges Christen holds the record for running with a table in his teeth 38 feet 8 inches. It might not sound like much, but let me repeat: he did it with his teeth, and on top of that there was a lady sitting on the table.

I can barely pick up a chair with my teeth and Grace points out that dragging it totally doesn't count.

The good thing is that a tooth that has been wobbly for weeks finally popped out.

SHARING A ROOM

Everyone in my family except Sharon shares a room, which is funny since Sharon's name has almost all the same letters as the word *share*. But she's really bad at it.

Mom and Dad share a room.

The twins share a room.

Maggie and Grace share a room.

Jake and I share a room. Actually, Jake is really bad at sharing, too. His idea of sharing is taking, and then destroying, like he did to my old tent. He cut it into pieces, taped them all over his body, and pretended to be a superhero called Seaweed.

Anyway, the main thing about sharing a room is that you never share anything else. I try to make it clear to him that he has one side of the room and I have the other. The things on his side are his. The things on my side are mine. And although this is a simple concept, it is hard for him to grasp. So I've stuck a line of tape down the middle of the room to help him.

"My bed is on this side, yours is on the other. Everything on this side is mine. Everything on your side is yours. I won't touch your stuff and you should never touch mine."

But I can't be in my room every second of the

day. I go to school. Jake does not. This leaves him with many opportunities to touch my things.

By "touch" I really mean destroy.

★ MY BIRTHDAY LIST #3 ★

1. A new tent. You know why.
2. A book about pigeons.
3. Luke Skywalker and Jar Jar Binks action figures. (You must remember that Jake ripped their heads off!)

THE BATHROOM

Sharon has the lead in her high school musical. I know this because she explains it to every single person she meets. "I have *the lead* in the high school musical. That means I'm the main person." She says this like she's the *only* person in the play. "We're doing *Oklahoma!*"

I have no idea about the musical until she starts practicing.

There's nothing like hearing the word *Oklahoma* sung over and over again to make your ears want to fall off, which must have been how the person who organized the world's loudest dog bark felt: 76 dogs howling at one time.

Although I know which one I'd pick to hear: the dogs.

One morning she announces in her sing-song way that the acoustics are best in the bathroom, so she'll be practicing in there from now on, and no one is to disturb her. Then she flounces upstairs. A few seconds later we hear: "OOOOOOOKLAHOMA!"

"She needs her privacy," Mom says.

Dad shrugs. "And it muffles the singing."

NOTHING FUNNY ABOUT PEE

Mom and Dad are watching the news, Grace is with them, Caitlin and Casey are doing homework in their room, Maggie is in her room probably doing sit-ups, and Sharon is enjoying the privacy of the bathroom. Jake is asleep. He can sleep through anything, even Sharon's singing.

I say good night, go upstairs, climb into bed, and pull out *The Guinness Book of World Records*, which is hard to concentrate on while "Oklahoma!" is sung again and again and again.

Strangely, I feel damp and cold, and there's a gross smell. I sniff my sheets, then throw myself out of bed and run downstairs.

I speak slowly so my parents get the full weight of what I am saying, especially because the news always distracts them. "He. Peed. In. My. Bed."

Grace responds in her typical way: falling on the floor laughing at me. "You lay down in pee-ee-ee-ee." She stretches this word out because she's laughing while she says it. She stops laughing for a second, sits up, and says in a fancy accent, "He peed in thee beed." She laughs more about her dumb rhyme.

"There is nothing funny about pee, Grace," I say. "Not lying in it or smelling it."

"You smelled pee," she squeaks.

Mom and Dad both smile a little at this.

"Mom, this is not funny!"

"Teddy, I'm sorry about the pee."

Grace takes a gulp of air. "The pee," she blurts out and then starts laughing again. She's laughing so hard she crawls out of the living room.

"Jake wanted to have his nap in your bed this afternoon. I forgot to change the sheets," Mom explains.

"Don't let him nap in my bed."

"It's just a little pee. I'll take care of it." We walk upstairs and she grabs a new set of sheets. I watch her closely as she changes them. "There, all clean," she whispers and pats the bed. "Teddy, I'm sorry, but Jake feels safe in your bed."

"If Jake feeling safe is so important, I'm sure your bed is as good as mine."

★ MY BIRTHDAY LIST #4 ★

1. A new tent.
2. A book about pigeons.
3. Luke Skywalker and Jar Jar Binks action figures. (You know why.)
4. A new pee-free bed. (You really know why.)

SCIENCE UNIT: BIRDS

"Pee!" Viva whispers. "Really?" We're studying birds now and Ms. Raffeli is having us draw our favorite. Viva is one good artist. Her eagle looks so real. My pigeon on the other hand looks like a pile of pudding. Lonnie is drawing an owl.

"Viva, I wasn't talking to you." This is becoming a habit of hers. A bad habit.

"I can't help it that Ms. Raffeli put us together."

Ms. Raffeli is big on cooperation, so our desks arc always clustered together instead of in rows.

"Use the Force, Teddy," Lonnie says. The Force comes more naturally to him. It doesn't seem to bother him that Viva's invading our space. Of course, Lonnie doesn't have five sisters and a little brother always badgering him.

Viva whispers, "What did your parents do? Did Jake get in trouble?"

I sigh because I know she will never give up.

"My mom changed the sheets. Besides that, they did nothing."

"Boy," Viva says. "Your life is really different from mine. I'm an only child. Every single thing I do is watched, noticed, commented on, and discussed. It's like living under a microscope."

"You want to trade?" I ask.

Ms. Raffeli circles our desks. "A little less talking, a little more drawing," she says.

That's fine with me.

THE LUNCHROOM

As soon as Lonnie and I sit down, Viva comes over and starts right where we left off.

"What about your family, Lonnie?"

"I've got an older brother. He's in the same grade as Teddy's sister Sharon."

"That must be nice," Viva says.

"You don't know Jerome," I say.

Lonnie rubs his arm where Jerome probably punched him. "Brothers are a pain."

Viva looks shocked. "Your brother hits you?"

"All siblings do it," Lonnie says. "Wait until you meet Teddy's sister Grace."

"It's true," I say. "Part of having sisters and

brothers is that they beat you up. You must know that."

"How many times do I have to say this?" Viva sighs. "My life is very different."

THE BATHROOM STRIKES BACK

Sharon taking over the upstairs bathroom is not a big deal because Dad is right about the singing being muffled, and also we have another bathroom.

So everything is fine until Jake is in the bathroom and has been in there for a long time. I guess I should be grateful that he's not using my bed, but I don't feel grateful. I feel like I'm going to explode.

"Jake, hurry up." I pound the door.

"Wait, Teddy," he shouts.

Dad walks by with a basket of laundry. "Jake's in the bathroom?" I nod. "That's great." My parents have been potty training him for years. He doesn't like to use the toilet. He's scared a hand will reach up and drag him down. (Thanks, Grace, for putting that idea in his head.)

"It's great except I have to go," I say, hopping from leg to leg.

Finally, Jake walks out. "It's all yours," he says,

just like Dad says it.

I do my thing and flush, but the water doesn't go down. So I flush again. Still it's not flushing like normal. So I flush one more time. Instead of the water going down the pipe, it rises up. Higher and higher, just like how I picture the largest bubble gum bubble growing and growing until it's 20 inches, which is big.

Now I'm freaking out and I'm pulling on the door but it won't open. This door always sticks. I look behind me. I pull on the door more because the toilet water doesn't stop when it's close to the top and it doesn't stop when it reaches the top.

It's really not stopping and I'm pulling on the door and I'm shouting "DAD!" just as the water pours out all over the floor.

"DAD!" I scream again. Toilet water drowns my shoes.

JAKE'S PUNISHMENT (OR NOT!)

After the plumber leaves, Dad has a talk with Jake. "There are only a few things that go into a toilet. Socks are not one of them."

"But I was keeping the hand from getting me."

"Jake, I promise there is no hand, and socks

don't go in toilets." Then he gives Jake a big hug.

"That's it?" I say. "If I dropped a sock down a toilet I'd never hear the end of it. Plus my sneakers were covered in pee water!"

"And I washed them," Dad says. "In the washing machine. Your sneakers are cleaner than most things in this house."

He's right of course. My sneakers are clean, but some things you can't get over.

"Teddy," Dad says. I think maybe he's about to offer to buy me a new pair. "Later I'll need help raking. Mr. Murney is complaining about the leaves."

And I'm complaining about my sneakers, but who listens to me?

★ MY BIRTHDAY LIST #5 ★

1. A new tent. (If Jake weren't around I would still have my old tent.)
2. A book about pigeons. (Really.)
3. Luke Skywalker and Jar Jar Binks action figures. (Only those ones.)
4. A new pee-free bed.
5. New sneakers. (I don't care what you say. I want new sneakers.)

GOOD LUCK

Lonnie and I hide behind a tree in my backyard, spying on Grumpy Pigeon Man. Except we can't see him. We think he's going to let the pigeons out and we don't want Grumpy Pigeon Man to catch us watching.

"Are you sure you don't smell pee on my shoes?" I whisper.

"It was a week ago, Teddy," he whispers back. "Your shoes stink, but it's the natural aroma of your feet."

"Pigeons!" Grumpy Pigeon Man calls. "Come on, pigeons!" He appears and opens the door to the screened-in section.

The pigeons flutter around first and then fly out. He makes his way back into his house, leaving the pigeons out in the sky. Alone.

We come out of hiding when he goes inside.

"They're so cool," I say. "They never bump into each other."

Lonnie nods. "It's like they're on a track."

"You two are nut-oes," Grace says, making us jump. She's right behind us. "How can you possibly like those things? They're ugly, dirty, and gross."

And as if to prove her point something plops on my head. A yellowish, whitish, brownish

goop drips down my fore-
head and slides onto my
nose. Grace doubles over
laughing.

"You know," Lonnie
says, "in some countries
getting pooed on is good
luck."

Grace laughs so hard she falls down.

RECORD ATTEMPT 5

"Raking the largest leaf pile is not a good world
record," I say. Lonnie and I are in the school
bathroom (the only place Viva can't interrupt us).

"What happened?" he asks.

"Wind," I say. "So much wind."

THE BOOK IS LOST

"Lonnie," Mom says. "I'm
so glad you could come over.
You want a snack?"

"Hi, Mrs. Mars."

"Mom, did you move
my book?" I'm looking for

The Guinness Book of World Records. Lonnie and I spend a lot of afternoons studying it.

"Why hello yourself! Such a polite son." I ignore her and her sarcasm.

"I left it here this morning." I point to the kitchen table.

"I didn't touch it," she says and puts out some milk and apples.

"Are you sure you didn't move it, Mom?"

"Check your room, Teddy. It's probably there."

I run upstairs. Jake's on his bed, drawing.

"Hey, Jake, have you seen my book?"

"Which book?" He keeps drawing.

"My book. *The Guinness Book of World Records.*" I look on my bed. "You know, that big book with gold letters." I look under my bed.

"Don't think so." He's still drawing. I look on my desk, then I look at Jake, who is still drawing. Drawing on a book, not on paper.

THE BOOK IS FOUND

He is drawing *on* it. He is drawing all *over* it. My *Guinness Book of World Records.* He is drawing a mustache on the smallest dog in the world (5.4 inches).

"Give me that!" I grab the book and flip through the pages. I cannot believe this. They are filled. He has drawn all over the book. There are pirate patches over eyes, Mohawks on heads, and extra antennae on everything else. "JAKE! This is mine." I run down the stairs. "Mom! Jake drew all over my book."

"Jake wouldn't do that."

I hold up the book. I fan the pages for emphasis. "Jake destroys everything!"

"He was so quiet," she says. "I thought he'd fallen asleep."

"The book is totally ruined."

"Not totally ruined. He didn't draw at all on

the words, just on the pictures."

"That's the best part! Lonnie, tell her that's the best part."

But Lonnie is looking past me and past my mom.

"Mrs. Mars," he says, "I think you should turn around." He points at the oven.

Both Mom and I turn to look. A cloud of smoke is pouring out.

"Oh phooey!" she says. "That's dinner burnt again." She pulls out the food and turns on the fan just as the smoke alarm blares. Mom tosses us dishcloths and says, "Wave them at the smoke alarm so it stops." Then she runs upstairs to Jake, who is wailing as loudly as the smoke alarm.

"Well, that's my problem forgotten about. Again!" I say, as Lonnie and I wave at the smoke alarm.

★ MY BIRTHDAY LIST #6 ★

1. A new tent. (Ruined by Jake a.k.a. The Destructor.)
2. A book about pigeons.

3. Luke Skywalker and Jar Jar Binks action figures. (Also ruined by The Destructor.)
4. A new pee-free bed. (The Destructor.)
5. New sneakers. (The Destructor.)
6. New *Guinness Book of World Records.* (And yes, one more time, The Destructor.)

RECORD ATTEMPT 6

"What in the world, Teddy?" Mom looks like her mouth is about to fall off her face.

"I was breaking a world record," I say, wiping my head with a towel.

"With eggs?"

"The most eggs cracked on the head."

"How could that possibly be a good idea?"

"It was Grace's," I say.

Grace stands next to me, trying to stifle her hysterics. "I didn't think he'd do it."

"So did you break a world record?" Mom asks.

"No, I don't think six eggs will break any record. I'd need a chicken factory. You wouldn't possibly buy me eighty dozen eggs?"

Mom shakes her head. "You missed a spot on the floor," she says as she walks out of the room.

NEVER TRY TO TALK TO A MOTHER

Unbelievable as it sounds, when I walk in from
school, the house is quiet and after a week the smoke
smell is finally gone. Mom is in the kitchen reading
the newspaper. And I know this is my chance.

"Mom—"

"Teddy, dear, Jake is having his first playdate
without me. No one else is home. Could you get
yourself a snack?" She goes back to reading.

I start over again. This is important. "Mom,
my birthday is tomorrow—"

"I know when your birthday is."

Clearly, I need to get to my point. "Don't let
Jake ruin it."

"Why would he do that?"

"Because he ruins everything. He's The Destructor. Every step he takes destroys a house, or a car, or a nine-year-old's life."

"Like the Blob," she says.

"I don't know the Blob."

"It's an old movie about this slow-moving blob from outer space that gobbles up everything in its path. And as it gobbles up more it grows bigger and bigger."

I pause and think about Jake being the Blob. She takes her glasses off and keeps talking. She's on a roll.

"Of course it's not simply Jake that's the Blob. It's this whole family. Gobbling me up in dishes, dirty laundry, homework, grocery shopping, and cooking, and right now I have five minutes to read this paper in peace and quiet before I am swallowed up again by the Blob. Do you see me complaining?"

I shake my head. "Jake is not a blob. He's not slow-moving. My point is, Mom, don't let him destroy my birthday."

"Teddy, nothing is going to destroy your birthday. You are going to have a great tenth birthday."

Mom puts on her glasses and goes back to her paper, just as Jake runs in and crashes into us.

"We made brownies, Mama! Brownies! There's enough for everyone except Teddy because Teddy doesn't like brownies."

I wouldn't eat them even if I liked them. I know where he puts his hands.

Mom sighs. "Let the Blob begin!"

"He's The Destructor," I say.

"What's a destructor?" Jake asks.

IT'S MY BIRTHDAY AND EVERYTHING IS A LITTLE TOO QUIET

It's my birthday. I am officially ten. TEN! TEN! TEN!

So here are my questions: Where's the smell of lemon cupcakes? Mom always makes them after we go to bed the night before our birthdays. She says it's too distracting if we're around. But this morning there's no smell.

And why is it so quiet? It's a school day and we all have to get ready, and on top of that, parents have to make pancakes. Presents have to be given. There needs to be some noise. But instead it's quiet. The lights are still off. Smarty Pants meows for her food. This has got to be a joke. They're going to surprise me.

"Mom? Dad?" I walk into their room. Jake is with them.

"Oh, Teddy." Mom rubs her eyes. She doesn't look so good. There's a bucket on the floor. "I'm so sorry. I feel—" She stops speaking, plugging her mouth with her hands like she's holding something down.

"Teddy—" Dad starts, but Jake wakes up.

"Dad, I don't feel good." And a geyser of liquid shoots out of his mouth all over Dad.

Sharon walks in. She is definitely not singing. She's carrying a trash can. It's full. "I feel awful," she moans.

Caitlin calls from her bed, "Mom! Help!"

Casey calls next. "Me too."

Maggie races down the stairs, heading for the other bathroom. Grace follows close behind.

Jake looks up for a second. "Happy birthday, Teddy," he says and then vomits some more.

SCHOOL LUNCH

"What's the deal with school lunch?" Lonnie asks. "You hate school lunch. You never have school lunch. And it's your birthday."

"The Destructor is the deal." I shake my head.

"What happened?" Lonnie asks.

"It's gross," I say.

"I can handle it."

"It's bad," I say.

"I'm sure I've heard worse," he says.

"Are you talking about vomit?" Viva leans over.

"How did you know that?"

"What's grosser than vomit?" she says.

"Is she right?" Lonnie asks.

"Yes. But it's not just a little vomit. Are you sure you can handle it?"

"Oh brother," Viva says. "Just tell the story. Knowing you, it'll be good."

So I tell the whole crazy story. "And it had to be from the dumb brownies because it's the only thing that everyone ate except me."

Turns out that Viva is not bothered by vomit. Lonnie gives me half of his lunch. "Think of it as a birthday present."

Before we get up for recess, Viva taps my elbow and passes me her cookies. "You totally deserve these more than me."

"Thanks," I say.

She shrugs, stands up, and walks out alone.

I admit, I don't need any more people in my life, but maybe she's not so bad.

"Wait up!" I yell, pulling Lonnie out of his seat and shoving the cookies in my mouth.

MY BIRTHDAY CONTINUES

After school I come home, where every person in my family has been hanging out all day.

I find Mom alone in the kitchen, sipping tea. When she sees me she starts to hug me, then stops. "I don't want to get you sick."

Dad comes in. "Oh, Teddy. We are so sorry. How was school?"

"Remarkably the same when you don't bring in a special birthday snack and the school lunch is corned beef hash, which you might remember is something I detest."

"I promise we'll make it up to you," Mom says. "Do you want to open presents?"

"What about dinner, and cupcakes, and ice cream?" I ask.

Mom and Dad look at each other and shiver like just thinking about food will make them throw up.

"We really didn't move from the sofa," Mom says. "But we do have leftovers and there are popsicles in the freezer." She smiles like this is a great adventure.

"Let's go into the living room," Dad says, clearly changing the subject. "You can open your presents, then decide about dinner."

We go in and there's Jake sitting in the middle of a pile of paper like he's floating on a cloud. It takes me a second but then I realize that paper is, in fact, wrapping paper—ripped-open wrapping paper and presents.

Presents that are mine!

He looks up. "Happy birthday, Teddy. Look!" He holds up the latest version of *The Guinness Book of World Records*. "And a tent!"

"You opened my presents?"

"Jake." Mom moves forward. "Those were Teddy's."

"I warned you, Mom."

"He didn't mean to," Dad says.

"No, he never means to." I grab the tent and my book. "I'll be in the backyard."

PUTTING UP THE TENT

Putting up a tent is harder than it looks. The directions are no help. I tossed them to the side a while ago. Dad came out and started telling me what to do and how to get it up and acting like nothing had happened. I sent him away. Then Mom tried. She looked like she was going to be sick all over the tent. I sent her back inside.

Next came Jake.

"I'm really, really, really, really sorry, Teddy."

He actually said it a million times more but you get the point. By now I had stuck all these long thin poles into these long thin holes in the tent. This was not easy, but at least with those poles in, the tent popped up and actually looked like a tent. This lasted for five seconds before Jake shouted, "COWABUNGA!" and dive-bombed it.

Do I need to say that the tent collapsed? Then, and don't ask me how, while I turned toward the house to yell to Mom and Dad, he pulled out all the poles I had put in and was pretending they were lightsabers.

"Look, Teddy," he hollered. "Look! I have the Force!"

As I drag Jake back into the house, I say to Dad, "For my birthday I want one thing: keep The Destructor away from me."

"What's The Destructor?" Jake asks. "Is it something from Star Wars?"

PUTTING UP THE TENT PART 2

And so now I'm starting again. I'm doing this totally by myself. I have made it perfectly clear to every member of my crazy family that I do not want their help (not that my sisters were offering).

I pick up four silver stakes (for the corners) and the hammer that Dad brought out just as Grumpy Pigeon Man's back door slams.

"Pigeons!" he calls like he's calling a dog. "Pigeons!"

I drop to the ground like a pancake. It's a dumb thing to do but I can't help it. This day has been bad enough without getting yelled at by him.

But now I'm stuck. There's only one choice: stay exactly where I am. I know I'm in plain sight but maybe if I don't move he won't see me.

He's lugging a bucket to the birdhouse. He moves slowly—like a snail, or a sloth.

At this rate I'll be here all night.

"Pigeons!" he calls again. The pigeons flutter and coo like they can't wait to see the guy, and then he disappears around the other side.

The coop is made up of two parts: a shed section and a screened-in section. I can't see inside the shed because there are no windows, but of course I can see inside the screened-in porch part.

I can't see the door that goes to the shed, but obviously there is one and there's also a door between the shed and the screened-in porch.

Grumpy Pigeon Man reappears in the screened-in part and pours water out of the bucket. He clucks at the birds, turns his bucket upside down, and sits.

For like ten minutes he sits there. Staring at

the pigeons. Seriously, he doesn't move. I almost wonder if he has died but then he sneezes.

I didn't think my birthday could get worse but it did. I'm hiding out from my neighbor who's staring at his pigeons. Sure, they're cool, and sure, it would be interesting to watch them that closely, but I've got a tent to put up before I turn eleven!

PUTTING UP THE TENT PART 3

Finally he stands up and seriously S-L-O-W-L-Y makes his way to the door. He must be the slowest guy in the world. This is not a category in *The Guinness Book of World Records*. YET. But Grumpy Pigeon Man could set the record for slowest human being.

Strange but true, there are two entries for slowest things. One is a plant that takes 80 to 150 years to bloom; the other is the blue whale, which has the slowest heartbeat of any mammal (four to eight beats a minute). Humans' have like 70 beats a minute.

There's no point watching him. It's too excruciating. So I close my eyes and count the seconds until I hear his door slam. I get to ninety-seven when someone hollers, "Hey, you!"

By *someone* I don't really mean *someone*. There is only one person who hollers like that.

I look up. Grumpy Pigeon Man is staring right at me over the fence. That guy is slow but of course he has eyes like a hawk. Why didn't I remember that?

"Yeah, you! Tent Boy!"

"Tent Boy?"

I look around hoping he's talking to someone else. He isn't. Even in this strange predicament, I know if Grace hears that nickname I'll never be called Teddy again.

"You've been lying on the ground ever since I came out. That tent isn't going to put itself up." He's old so he's allowed to be rude. I'm only ten so I'm not.

"When I was your age I could put up and take down a tent in less than two minutes." I stand up. There's no point in hiding now. "You're slower than molasses, Tent Boy."

"Thank you, sir." I pick up the hammer and the stakes. Maybe if I start again, he'll go away.

"Why are you putting it up anyway?" he grumps.

I don't know why but I answer the guy. "It's my birthday." Then I say (and I do not know where this crazy idea comes from), "Starting today, I'm living in this tent."

Grumpy Pigeon Man nods. "Makes sense. Only pigeons are crazy enough to actually like living with so many." He lopes away. At his back door he calls out, "Hey, Tent Boy!"

I cringe and look around. But Grace is nowhere to be seen. "You'll never get it up that way. You've got to start with the poles. End with the stakes."

THE TENT IS UP

I did it. My tent is up and perfectly located. It's not too far away from the house, but far enough. I can also see and hear the pigeons, and except for the fact that my backyard is actually a hill, it's really comfortable.

I bring out pillows, blankets, and my old copy of *The Guinness Book of World Records*. I already have my new one with me. I like comparing them.

It's not like the new one is better than the old one, just different. It's got different categories, different pictures, even different records. For example the new one doesn't have the record for the dog that holds the most tennis balls in his mouth (5). Anyway, I hang out for a long time reading them. I like it out here. For one thing The Destructor is nowhere near me.

In the morning I'll tell my parents I'm not moving back inside. They think tonight is just special.

"Happy birthday, Teddy," I say. The pigeons coo back. Obviously, they think it's special, too.

"I HAVE GOT TO TAKE A PICTURE OF THIS!"

That's how Grace wakes me. She's got her phone in my face and she's laughing her head off.

"You've never been into photography," I say.

"Mom's wanted me to have a hobby for years. I've finally found it. Now, stand outside so I can get one of you next to the tent."

Normally I wouldn't do anything she suggested, but she's very convincing. Especially when she's twisting my arm.

"Say cheese!"

THE BEST THING

"You slept in a tent on your birthday?" Again, Viva's sandwich freezes in midair. Again, it's the only thing not moving in this whole room. And again, I wish she'd leave me alone.

The lunchroom is so loud that I was positive I could have a private conversation with Lonnie. A lot has happened since yesterday and I want to fill him in. But I was wrong. Viva is definitely Yoda. She's got the Force and the ears.

"You slept in a tent on your birthday?" she repeats. "Why?"

There are so many things that Viva doesn't understand about my family and my life, and I can't begin to explain them to her. I don't want to explain them to her. I'm about to tell her to sit somewhere else when Lonnie smiles. Darn Jedi warrior.

I take a breath and tell them both about what happened when I got home yesterday: no birthday dinner, no cupcakes, no ice cream, and The Destructor opened my presents.

"Oh brother!" Viva says.

"That is wrong," Lonnie says.

"So wrong," Viva says, then asks, "What did you do?"

"I put up the tent," I say. "There's loads of room inside it. And tonight I'll sleep with my feet facing down the hill, which ought to take care of the sliding problem I had last night."

"You're going to sleep in it again?" Lonnie asks.

"This is what I wanted to tell you." I stop talking and look at Viva. "I'll tell you later, Lonnie."

"Aw, come on!" Viva throws down her sandwich. "Look, I'm not going to say anything. Who can I tell? I'm not friends with anyone else."

Lonnie looks at me, shakes his head, then says, "I think she's right."

"Fine, but if I hear one word about this, I'll know who's to blame."

"I promise."

"I'm staying in the tent."

Lonnie looks at me like, what's the big deal? "We know you're staying in the tent."

"No, no, I mean I've moved into the tent. I'm going to live in the tent. Full-time."

"You can't live in a tent!" Viva says.

"My mom says as long as I do my homework and keep it clean, it's fine with her."

"That's ridiculous!" Viva sputters. "Kids don't live in tents. My parents would never let me live in a tent."

"Man, you have the life." Lonnie gives me a high five. "Your parents are so outnumbered they give up." He says this like it's the best thing in the world, like I broke some kind of world record.

REASONS WHY LIVING IN A TENT IS EASY

1. It's my own space. Shared with no one.
2. I'm not scared of a little noise like some kids are. I know it's probably just a skunk. Skunks aren't bad. They only stink you if you scare them, and I'm not going to do that. It could be a raccoon. Raccoons are okay unless they're rabid. That would be bad, but not as bad as lying in a bathtub with 87 rattlesnakes. Jackie Bibby did that to get into *The Guinness Book of World Records*.
3. Again, I don't have a third point. I've got to work on this or Ms. Raffeli will kill me.

SPEAKING OF MS. RAFFELI

Speaking of Ms. Raffeli, she found out I was living in a tent. Mom told her. I heard her on the phone.

That day at school, Ms. Raffeli said to me, "Somehow I'm not surprised." Then she said almost the exact same thing Mom did: "As long as you do your homework and stay clean, you could sleep in a bucket and I wouldn't be bothered."

The Destructor isn't happy about it though.

He keeps asking when I'm moving back into our room. I refuse to talk to him, but if I were talking to him I'd tell him I'm staying in the tent forever.

Each night I climb in, shake out my blankets (you never know what might have crawled in), zip my tent closed, and relax.

Tonight I can't help thinking about 87 rattlesnakes slithering all over me. It would be pretty loud with all that hissing and rattling, but it would still have to be quieter than the racket coming from my house. No wonder Grumpy Pigeon Man doesn't like us.

PIGEON DETECTIVE

For my birthday, Lonnie gave me the two new Star Wars action figures I wanted. Obviously, I didn't get the new sneakers or a new bed. No one gave me a book about pigeons, which is a problem since that's what I picked for my school report.

But because I live in my backyard, next door to a pigeon coop, I've decided to take things into my own hands.

THINGS I KNOW ABOUT PIGEONS

It's lucky for me that the pigeons have that screened-in part of the coop or else I wouldn't know anything. A lot of what goes on happens out there.

1. Grumpy Pigeon Man feeds them twice a day. Once really early in the morning (he wakes me up) and again in the afternoon (after I get home from school).
2. When Grumpy Pigeon Man lets them out, he doesn't feed them until they come back.
3. Sorry, Ms. Raffeli.

THINGS I DON'T KNOW ABOUT PIGEONS

Ms. Raffeli says a good scientist always asks questions (this is of course true for detectives too) so here are a few:

1. When they fly free, how do they know it's time to all come home together?
2. What goes on in the part of the coop that looks like a shed and I can't see into?
3. Another apology, Ms. Raffeli.

TENT LIFE

I still eat in the house and use the bathroom. But the rest of the time I'm out here. I have everything I need: snacks, which I keep in a container (I don't want animals roaming in), flashlight, notebook, pencils, pencil sharpener, erasers, markers, books, clothes, pillows, sleeping pad, and blankets. The nights are getting cooler so I keep adding blankets.

Tonight Dad shows up. "How's it going?" he asks as he ducks down into the tent.

"It's good, Dad." I offer him an Oreo, the only chocolate I like.

"When are you moving back into the house, Teddy?"

"I like it here."

"I know Jake drives you crazy but you can't live in the backyard forever."

"Those pigeons do."

"You're not a pigeon, Teddy."

"I'm staying, Dad."

"Well, we miss you."

"Hey, Dad?"

"Yeah?"

"Don't tell Mom about the Oreos. I didn't ask if I could have them."

He smiles and grabs two more before ducking out of the tent.

TENT BOY

"Tent Boy!" Grumpy Pigeon Man yells. "Tent Boy!"

I guess it was only a matter of time before he yelled at me, but I didn't think it would be first thing in the morning and I hoped he'd use my real name!

I'm already dressed, have had breakfast, and am hanging out reading *The Guinness Book of World Records* before it's time for school, but still!

I poke my head out of the tent. "My name is Teddy."

He leans over the fence. "You got that tent up. Finally."

"Yes, sir."

"You want to make some money? Get yourself some better digs?"

"Better digs?" I don't understand him.

"A better home, you numbskull."

"I like my home."

Grumpy Pigeon Man sighs and sounds like our cat sneezing. "Do you want to earn some money or not?"

I finally understand what he's getting at. "Yes,

sir. I need a lamp so I can read at night. Holding a flashlight in one hand and a book in the other is harder than it looks."

He sighs again. The resemblance to Smarty Pants is uncanny. "Get yourself over here, Tent Boy."

MY NEW JOB: INSIDE THE PIGEON COOP

"I've never been inside a pigeon coop," I say.

"It's an aviary, Tent Boy."

"An aviary," I say. "That's a much cooler word than coop or birdhouse. But I guess birdhouses are usually smaller. But technically this is a bird house."

"Do you always talk this much?"

"I don't know how to answer that, sir. If I answer, I'm talking, and clearly you want me to be quiet, but if I don't answer you'll think I wasn't listening."

"Pigeons like quiet," Grumpy Pigeon Man grumps. "If you can't be quiet you can't have the job, Tent Boy."

"Teddy," I remind him.

"Sure, Tent Boy. Follow me." We go around

to the side of the shed I've never seen. There is a door, just like I thought, but also two windows on either side of the door. He opens it and we step inside. "Always close this door."

"I can do that. Not a problem. I close doors all the time—" Then I stop because it's so quiet. It's quiet like the grown-ups' library is and seriously like my house never is. The birds scratch and coo. Their feathers make a soft sound that matches their voices.

The room is made of wood. One wall is covered with wooden cubes that some pigeons are sitting in. Some are fluffing themselves, some are sleeping. There aren't any cages or anything.

"They look like the cubbies we had in kindergarten," I whisper.

"They're nesting boxes, not cubbies."

"Nesting boxes," I repeat. "That is a cooler word than cubbies."

He opens a big bin. "This is their food."

I point to a door. "That must go into the porch."

"It's called a loft, and before you say anything, it is a cooler word than what you called it."

MY NEW JOB PART 2:
INSIDE THE PORCH (I MEAN LOFT)

We walk through and are now in the loft, which is a cool word.

It's screened in on every side, and there is a door to get out. From here, I can see my tent, backyard, and house. I can also see Grumpy

Pigeon Man's house and his back door. "Except for the pigeons this is like my gran's porch."

"Loft, Tent Boy, loft," Grumpy Pigeon Man says. "Twice a day you'll feed them. They eat for ten minutes, then you take the seed away. This door is only used to let the birds out for exercise."

We walk back into the aviary and he shows me a long rectangular tray made of wood, with a roof and wooden bars across it. "This is for their food." He points to something that looks like a rocket but with holes around the bottom. "This is for water. And that"— he nods toward a shallow metal bowl—"is for their baths."

"They bathe in a bowl?" I ask.

"What else would they bathe in? A hot tub?" He walks out of the aviary. I follow. "Didn't I say close the door?"

I nod.

"So do it."

He points to a bucket and a spigot that's attached to his house. "You change their water and clean their bathing bowl here."

"Got it."

"Lastly, don't think that because you're working here you can invite anyone into the aviary. These birds are not toys. Is that clear?"

"Yes, sir."

"I'm giving you the rest of today off. I'll expect you tomorrow morning at five thirty."

"That's early."

"Do you want the job, Tent Boy?"

"I'll see you tomorrow, sir." As I walk away I picture my first paycheck going to an alarm clock. I might even have to get an advance from my parents.

ALARM CLOCK: THE QUEST

"Oh brother," Viva whispers across the table. "Who gets up at five thirty to feed pigeons?"

Viva works on her eagle, which is mid-dive, claws outstretched about to catch its prey. Lonnie's owl is looking very cool perched in its tree. I feel like I could touch his feathers. My pigeon, on the other hand, is definitely not looking as noble as I would like.

"No wonder the guy is so grumpy," Lonnie says. "He needs more sleep."

Viva laughs. "You must like pigeons a lot to get up so early."

"All I know is I need an alarm clock."

"Why did you say yes?" Lonnie asks.

"Try saying no to that guy." Which is true, but it's also true that I can't believe he asked me. He could've asked anyone. I've got a lot of sisters. On top of that, I finally have two things that are just mine: the tent and this job.

"I want to see inside the coop," Viva says. "When are you inviting us over?"

"Aviary," I say. "And never. Grumpy Pigeon Man made it clear."

"I don't want to get on his bad side." Lonnie shivers.

"What's so scary about this guy?" Viva asks.

Before I can answer, Ms. Raffeli appears at our desks. "A little less talking and a little more drawing. And Teddy, what happened to your pigeon? It looks like it's been through a war."

I wait for her to move on to another group. "There isn't anything scarier than a Grumpy Pigeon Man, which is why I need an alarm clock, and I need it tonight. The chances of me waking up without it are as likely as seeing a giant squid in the ocean."

Viva looks confused.

"*The Guinness Book of World Records*?" Lonnie asks.

I nod. "Largest creature *never* spotted in its

natural habitat."

"I can't help you," Lonnie says. "My clock plugs into the wall and you don't have electricity in your tent."

Viva shrugs. "My mom still wakes me. Maybe you could get yours to wake you."

"Viva, you've got to remember you're an only child," Lonnie says. "Teddy's mom would wake him about the same day those scientists find the giant squid."

Boy, is he ever right.

ALARM CLOCK: THE QUEST PART 2

After school, I drop my backpack and head for the kitchen. I've got to find an alarm clock or I'll lose my job before I work one day.

Mom is doing dishes. The Destructor sits in his cat box, looking through my old copy of *The Guinness Book of World Records*. The one he destroyed. "Hi, Teddy." He waves to me. I'm still mad at him so I ignore him.

"Hey, Mom—"

"Jake said hi to you," Mom interrupts.

"Hi, Destructor," I say.

"His name is Jake," she says.

I ignore her. "Mom, I need your help. You know Grumpy Pigeon Man hired me—"

"Mr. Marney," she interrupts.

"You know Mr. Marney hired me to feed his pigeons. He's going to pay me."

Grace walks in and stomps on my foot.

"Ouch!" Of course she ignores my suffering, and so does Mom.

"You're working for Grumpy Pigeon Man?" Grace asks.

"Mr. Marney," Mom says.

"Gross. You'll be totally covered in pigeon poo."

"Who's covered in pigeon poo?" Sharon asks as she walks in, for once not practicing for her musical. "Don't tell me it's some weirdo in this room. I have a hard enough time being a part of this family without being made fun of because someone is covered in pigeon poo."

Maggie hops into the kitchen, pulling on her sneakers. "Pigeon poo isn't so bad. It's good luck if a pigeon poos on you. Everyone knows that."

Grace snorts. "Teddy knows that. Your life really changed the day you got pooed on, right Teddy?"

"I am not going to be pooed on. Mom!"

"Of course you're not going to be pooed on. Everyone leave Teddy alone. Just make sure you take your shoes off before you come in the house. There could be poo on *them*."

ALARM CLOCK: THE QUEST PART 3

"I don't believe this!" I say. "Look, Mom, I need an alarm clock. I've got to be there at five thirty tomorrow morning. Do you have one?"

"We do, but your father and I use it."

"I have to get up, Mom," I say.

And maybe to make up for the disastrous birthday she says, "I'm sure we can get a clock before tomorrow."

"Mom," Maggie interrupts, "you said you'd drive me to practice today. Come on."

"I'll pick it up on my way back," she says.

"Thanks, Mom," I say just as Caitlin and Casey crash into the house and the phone starts ringing. They are moving fast across the kitchen and they both lunge for it. But Mom is faster than she looks. She's also got this thing called telepathy where she knows stuff without being told. She could tell there was someone on that phone she needed to talk to.

"Yes. Yes. What?" she says. "No! No! Of course, Principal Lawrence." Caitlin and Casey are super quiet during this exchange. Mom hangs up.

"Unbelievable! I have nothing to say, but this is not the end of it." She looks like she's about to scream her head off but instead she points up the stairs, sign language for: go to your room and if you speak one single word you'll be sorry. They read this loud and clear.

Mauna Loa in Hawaii is the world's largest active volcano. That means it still erupts, but not often. The last time was 1984. Mom is like that. She doesn't blow her top a lot but when she does it's big and it's best to stay back. The problem is I really need that alarm clock.

"So can you still get that clock today?" I ask.

"OUT!" she yells, waving a wooden spoon. "EVERYBODY OUT!"

It's like we all see the lava and run.

MY ALARM CLOCK

Dad says his cell phone is too important and if something happened to it he'd be up a creek without a paddle. So he gives me an old watch of his. "It doesn't have an alarm but at least you'll know what time it is when you do wake up. Be sure it doesn't get pooed on."

"Ha, ha," I say. "But I don't see how knowing the time without the alarm is going to help."

"It's the best I can do tonight."

"Mom said she'd get me an alarm clock."

"The twins distracted us. Congratulations on the job and good luck. You're braver than I am."

So I go to sleep wondering what the heck I'm doing working for Grumpy Pigeon Man, and at the same time just hoping I wake up.

FIRST DAY

"Tent Boy! Tent Boy!" Grumpy Pigeon Man yells at me. In my dream I'm one of his pigeons and I've just pooed all over Jake. "Tent Boy! Wake up!" I sit up, startled, and unzip the tent. Grumpy Pigeon Man is actually waking me up. He's not in my tent, but he's calling across the fence. "I'm awake," I say.

"Hurry up. If you want this job you have two minutes to get over here."

I can't believe it. Grumpy Pigeon Man is my alarm clock! I never thought he'd do that.

I still need to get one though. The chances that he'll stay my alarm clock are as good as me beating the record for the largest rubber duck collection (5,631).

There's no way it'll happen.

FIRST DAY PART 2

"Not like that," Grumpy Pigeon Man barks. "Like this." "Not that much food." "The food goes in the tray, not on the floor." "Ten minutes is up." "Don't spill the water." "Take it away." "Clean out that dish." "Watch what you're doing." "Don't scare the pigeons." "Close the door." "Don't slam it, Tent Boy."

Orders pour out of Grumpy Pigeon Man like the 120 million (seriously 120 million) red crabs that pour out of their burrows once a year on Christmas Island, the record for highest crab density. (You don't want to know why.)

I walk back to my tent wondering why I thought working for Grumpy Pigeon Man was a good idea. It's safe to say, I'm the only one in my family dumb enough to say yes. For a second, I think about The Destructor, and about how mad I get at him sometimes.

But before the thought sinks in my brain, I look up to see him running straight at me. His arms are stretched wide. "TEDDY!" he hollers. "I miiiissss youuuu!!!" He throws himself into my arms. I topple over backward and land straight onto my tent. It collapses and stays that way even when I push The Destructor off.

"He just wanted to give you a hug," Dad says later. I don't say a word. He stands around watching me put up the tent and tries again. "I'm glad the tent's not broken."

I nod as I put it up for what feels like the millionth time.

GRACE'S PROOF

Grace unzips my tent and sticks her head in. "Do you realize you've lived in this tent for twenty-two days?" She holds up her phone and clicks.

"Leave me alone, Grace."

"Never. It's the only proof I have. No one in my class believes that I have such a nut-o for a brother without the pictures." She zips up my tent and then says, "I'll be back."

If only I could figure out how to prove that she's a nut-o.

IT'S OFFICIAL

Every day Lonnie asks me what it's like to work for Grumpy Pigeon Man. Viva, of course, badgers me too, not only for information but also to invite them over so she can experience the pigeons firsthand.

(Her words, not mine.)

For some reason I haven't talked about my first week. Not even to Lonnie. I just needed to get through it, and now I have.

"Strange but true," I say, "this week could only have been worse if I was Wim Hof and spent 1 hour and 52 minutes 42 seconds buried up to my neck in ice."

Lonnie takes a bite out of his sandwich. "Was it as bad as eating 35,000 scorpions like Rene Alvarenga?"

"Maybe not that bad."

Viva leans in. "As bad as stuffing 400 drinking straws in your mouth. That has got to hurt."

Lonnie and I freeze. I'm pretty sure our eyes pop out, definitely not as far as Kim Goodman, whose eyes pop out from her head 0.47 inches, which might not seem like a lot but look at the picture and you know it is. "When did you start following *The Guinness Book of World Records*?" I ask.

"I always have." She snorts. "You don't own the exclusive rights to it."

"I know. I just didn't know you liked it."

"I've been reading it since I was five."

"It's official," Lonnie says.

"What?" I ask.

"She's one of us." Lonnie has always been generous that way. He's never been an excluder. He says it's not the Jedi way.

"What about Star Wars?" I ask. "Doesn't she have to pass some Star Wars test?"

"You think I don't know Star Wars?" she says. "Ask me."

Lonnie smiles and says. "R2-D2 and C-3PO are inspired by which actors?"

"Laurel and Hardy." She turns to me and waits for my question.

"What vegetable was used in the asteroid scene in *The Empire Strikes Back*?"

"That's easy, a potato." She turns back to Lonnie.

He thinks and then asks, "Which Kenner action figures never came out?"

"Aunt Beru and Uncle Owen Lars."

Lonnie says, "The Force is clearly with her."

"Fine," I say. Viva is still annoying, but she's grown on me, sort of like the record for tallest stack of pancakes (2 feet 6 inches).

Viva shrugs. "I'm glad you two finally realized it. So when can I get to meet these pigeons?"

THE TWINS

Nothing's a secret in our family. The walls are pretty much as thin as my tent.

Caitlin and Casey pretended to be each other at school. All day long Caitlin went to Casey's classes and all day long Casey went to Caitlin's classes. It wasn't until sixth period that they got caught. Turns out Caitlin is better at math. Grace tells me all of this when she comes outside to take her weekly picture of me.

The twins switched at school once before, when they were eight. They didn't get into trouble that time because they were so little. I wonder what will happen now that they're fourteen?

RECORD ATTEMPT 7

The fastest time to push an orange for a mile with the nose is 24 minutes and 36 seconds. This is a record I can beat.

Of course, to get to a mile in our kitchen means

going back and forth a bunch of times, but that's okay. I measured it and 352 times doesn't sound too bad.

FAILED ATTEMPT 7

I wasn't prepared for all the dust up my nose. Clearly the guy who broke that record was on a much cleaner floor than mine. It's been hours and my nose still feels itchy.

THE NIGHT BEFORE HALLOWEEN

"Don't make me do it, Dad," I say. "Please!"

"We talked about this before, Teddy. Either Jake trick-or-treats with you or you don't go. Mom is visiting Gran for two days. Sharon has a rehearsal. I'm taking Maggie and five other girls to the soccer game and we won't get back until late. Grace's going with the Van Epps. Anyway,

Lonnie will be with you, and his mom will be here until I get back."

"What about Caitlin and Casey? Why don't they take him?"

"They're still grounded for that stunt they pulled at school," Dad says. "And to be perfectly honest, I don't trust them."

"Oh great," I say. "So if I was less trustworthy I could have a Destructor-free Halloween?"

"You'll be fine, Teddy. All you have to do is walk him to a few doors, get some candy, and bring him home. Lonnie's mom will stay with him while you and Lonnie go back out. I'll be home in time to put him to bed. And here's his costume." Dad hands me a box with a hole cut in the bottom and another cut in the front. It looks remarkably like a cat box.

"What is he going as?" I ask.

"A cat in a cat box." Dad tries to keep a straight face when he says this. "Just draw some whiskers on his face, pink up his nose, and have him climb in. People will love it."

"People will love it? It's not even scary. I can't believe you are making me do this!"

"Sometimes we all have to help out the Mars Menagerie."

"Sometimes it would be nice if it were someone else helping besides me!"

HALLOWEEN MORNING

"This will be the worst Halloween ever." I don't even keep my voice down during class I'm so mad. Who cares if Ms. Raffeli looks over at me with those eyebrows? I'm getting used to grouchy grown-ups. I mean, Grumpy Pigeon Man grumbles at me every morning about his pigeons. That guy has got to learn to give a compliment every once in a while!

"At least you guys go together," Viva says. "I always have to be with my dad. It's so embarrassing."

"Come with us," Lonnie says right away.

"Really?" Viva sits up. She looks genuinely excited.

"You might want to think about this," I say. "Trick-or-treating with your parents is bad, but going with my brother is worse."

Lonnie ignores my comment. "Meet us at Teddy's house at five o'clock."

Viva smiles. "I'd have to ask my parents. And you know they'll call your dad and check on everything. They ask about a billion questions whenever I go to someone's house. Even so, my dad still might come." She laughs when she says this, but her face is red, which makes me think being an only child isn't always wonderful. "Oh, and my costume's not so good either."

"With a brother like mine, no one will even pay attention to you. I promise."

Ms. Raffeli shows up at our desks and all conversation stops.

COSTUME MISHAPS

Viva was right about her parents calling and checking on us. They really gave Dad the third degree but they finally agreed she could come.

Because Mom's not here and Dad spent all his time making the cat box costume, Lonnie and I are stuck in the same costumes we've been in for three years. I mean, our robes are so short our legs stick out. Darth Maul does not wear sneakers, or if he does, no one sees them. But everyone can see ours. And Mom wasn't there to do our face paint. Nothing against Lonnie's mom, but she wouldn't do the Darth Maul face. "It freaks me out too much," she said. So we had to do it ourselves.

"I don't mind being matching Darth Mauls again," Lonnie says. "He's creepy."

"Not after three years. I want to be something else. Something scarier."

"What's scarier than Darth Maul?"

"A 5 pound 3 ounce hair ball removed from someone's stomach seems pretty horrific. The white shark is the most dangerous shark in the world. That would have been a good costume. I would have even settled for the gaboon viper, which happens to be the snake with the longest fangs."

The Destructor looks up from out of his cat box costume. "I think you look scary."

"You live in a cat box most of your life," I say. "I'm not sure about your opinion."

Lonnie shakes his head, and then says, "First off, we couldn't have made any of those costumes, and second off, you're just mad because you got stuck with your little brother. But think about it, it's got to be better than the time Jerome took us."

"Wait till tonight is over, Lonnie, then you'll know. There's really no comparison."

YOU CALL THAT A BAD COSTUME?

"I'll get it!" The Destructor screams and charges to the door. He opens it. Standing there is the creepiest skin-dripping-off-bones, guts-spewing-out-from-the-neck zombie creature.

"AHHHH!" he wails and runs back to me. I understand his reaction. There is no category for scariest costume in *The Guinness Book of World Records* but if there were this one would win. It looks so real.

"Hey, Lonnie," the zombie creature says. "Hey, Teddy."

"Viva?" Lonnie asks.

"Yeah." She nods.

I can't believe it. It's Viva. Viva is in the best costume I have ever seen.

"Is this your little brother?" she asks. "Like I need to ask. Nice cat box."

"That's Viva?" The Destructor says. His voice is full of awe. I understand why.

"Seriously creepy," Lonnie says. "I don't even recognize you."

"My mom and dad did it. They love Halloween."

"I thought you said you wouldn't have a good costume?" I say.

"This is nothing compared to last year's."

"The face paint is outstanding," Lonnie says.

"They get this professional stuff. They also make molds for the fake skin."

Now I want to get Halloween over with even more than I did before Viva showed up. "Let's get going," I say. No one listens.

"You look incredible," Lonnie says.

"You guys look good too," she says. "Who did your faces?"

"Come on," I say. "Let's go before the candy runs out." That gets their attention.

REVENGE

The rest of the night is pretty much as I expected. Every house oohs and aahs over Viva's costume and thinks The Destructor is adorable and says nothing to Lonnie and me.

The Destructor also pulls me down the street, charges up to every door, grabs fistfuls of candy, never says trick-or-treat or thank you, complains that he's tired, but whines at the top of his voice when I suggest we take him home.

So we keep going.

We do not stop at Grumpy Pigeon Man's house. Of course his lights are on, but I don't even bother.

I know I shouldn't, but I let The Destructor eat as much candy as he wants. I doubt my father will ever ask me to take him out for Halloween again.

RECORD ATTEMPT 8

The month of October was a real washout in terms of breaking a world record. But I've got a new idea. Rubber bands. Shay Horay (Rubberband Boy, as he is called) got the record for stretching 78 rubber bands over his face in one minute. I seriously think I can beat this record.

"Lonnie, you're in charge of timing me."

"Ready when you are," he says.

The one hundred rubber bands that I got from Mom's desk are all laid out so they're easy to pick up. I really thought this record through and am sure I'm going to break it.

"Ready. Set. GO!" I say. I grab a rubber band

and stretch it over my face. I've put on about twenty-five when Lonnie shouts, "Thirty more seconds!"

There are three things I can't fathom.

1. How slow I am at getting these on—I'm not even halfway!
2. How painful rubber bands on the face actually are. They tug at your skin, your hair, your lips.
3. I'm actually in so much pain I forgot my third point.

But I don't stop. Maybe I can still make it.

"One minute!" Lonnie shouts. "Stop!"

Lonnie stares at me. "Wow, you're as ugly as an Acklay, an Acklay without teeth that is. Make that an Acklay without teeth after Obi-Wan Kenobi kills it."

"I can't see a thing, Lonnie. Get me out of here. Seriously. Help."

FAILED ATTEMPT 8

Besides Mom having to cut me out of the rubber bands, and my hair getting tangled in them so she had to chop it off in a bunch of places, and of course the fact that my face still has rubber band marks all over it after two days, it wasn't so bad.

This must mean I'm getting closer to breaking a record.

YOU NUT-O

"A month," Grace says.

"A month what?" I ask.

"A month! You nut-o! Do I really have to spell it out for you? Really?"

I can tell she's waiting for an answer but just for the fun of it I don't give her one. "You've lived out here for a month! Now don't move. The last picture was blurry."

Click!

THE DESTRUCTOR'S BEEN TRYING

The Destructor's been trying to move in with me ever since I moved out.

"No way," I say. And for once, Mom backs me up.

When it's time to go to bed Jake cries, "Teddy!" in this way like I'm never coming back.

"It's okay, Destructor," I say. "I'll see you in the morning." Then he holds me so tight I think tooth-paste might squeeze out of me.

I DON'T KNOW WHY

I don't know why but Grumpy Pigeon Man still wakes me up every morning. Of course, my parents have not bought me an alarm clock. The chances of that happening are about as good as me getting into *The Guinness Book of World Records*.

Anyway, I don't know why Grumpy Pigeon Man wakes me and I don't know why he wants me to take care of his birds. He still stays with me the whole time and still grumbles about every-thing I do wrong.

He could do it himself. He's slow but the pigeons don't care. They're on pigeon time. I ask him why he needs my help, but he never answers. So I keep showing up.

For some reason I can't help thinking about this monk who lived a long time ago (386–459 CE) but is in *The Guinness Book of World Records* anyway because he sat on a stone pillar for 39 years. You know *that* was uncomfortable.

Mom says some things aren't comfortable or easy, like having seven children, but you still do them.

After that Blob business I've stopped listening to her because what she says is just weird, but she might have a point.

TRASH DUTY

"Trash duty?" the twins sputter.

"Trash duty," Dad repeats. Apparently, being grounded wasn't enough of a punishment because the twins switched places again the day after Halloween. "You both will be on trash duty at school. For the next six weeks, you'll be cleaning up the school grounds."

"SIX WEEKS?" they gasp.

"Six weeks," Mom and Dad repeat.

"At school?"

"At school."

PIGEON FACTS

Unbelievable as it is, we are still studying birds. Maybe this unit will last forever.

"It doesn't normally last this long," Ms. Raffeli says. "But with all the new state standards I'm supposed to teach, everything takes longer."

Finally, we begin writing our reports on birds. The school library didn't have one single book about pigeons so Mom had to take me to the city library. It turns out there are about as many books on pigeons as there are world records. Who knew there was so much to say about pigeons?

Most of the books are boring and confusing and explain what to do if your pigeon ever gets some weird pigeon disease. But I did find one that didn't put me to sleep and that I could understand.

1. There are over two hundred breeds of pigeons!

2. Tumblers and rollers are pigeons that

somersault and flip in the air. Really.
They fly up and then flip as they fly.
3. I'm still reading, so no third fact yet.

THE DESTRUCTOR VS. THE SOCCER GAME

Maggie has a big soccer game today. Her team is in the finals. It's all very serious with coaches screaming out orders and referees in black and white running up and down the field.

Our whole family is here. Of course, we were late so we're all squished together in the last remaining spot on the bleachers. Lonnie's with us too because he's basically family, and what's one more kid to my parents?

We're having a really great time. It's cold outside so it's not so bad sitting close. And we're eating food like hot dogs and potato chips, stuff we never get to have. Sharon is singing the school song at the top of her lungs and it sounds surprisingly good.

Even The Destructor is acting normal. He's sitting on Mom's lap (not huddling under her legs like usual or running around bothering other families, tipping over their food and drinks).

We all start clapping and pounding our feet

and shouting out, "M-A-G-G-I-E! M-A-G-G-I-E! M-A-G-G-I-E! MMMMMMAGGIE!!!!!" And people around us start to do it too. "M-A-G-G-I-E! M-A-G-G-I-E! M-A-G-G-I-E! MMMMMMMMAGGIE!!!!!"

Maggie is center forward. She's incredible. She runs all over the field, chasing down the ball, passing it, even scoring. And then in the middle of this great feeling, I look around and I know something is wrong, someone is missing, and it's not Maggie, who's playing in the game.

Instantly, the sounds shift from exuberant

screams to almost silence. All the fun and great-
ness suddenly whooshes away and on the field I
see this little blip chasing Maggie. Maybe a dog?
I hope a dog. Of course it's not a dog.

Then I hear Mom say, "Oh no."

And at exactly the same time Dad says, "It's
Jake."

Well, I can tell you people were not happy about
a little brother running onto the field in the middle of the game, stealing the ball, and stopping the
play. It wasn't funny to anyone. We were asked to
take him home and keep him there until he could
follow the rules. And the referees and coaches all
had to meet and decide where play should start
again and how to handle the situation.

The one time we were all having fun, and The Destructor attacks again. For once I didn't think he would. But he did.

On top of it all, Maggie's team lost.

BACK TO NORMAL

"He ran out on the field?" Viva asks.

"In the middle of the game," Lonnie says.

"Oh brother, then what happened?"

"You mean after the referee yelled at my parents? Maggie ran home and isn't speaking to anyone. Sharon declared no one is invited to see her musical and isn't speaking to anyone but is still singing. The twins aren't speaking to anyone because they're still mad about picking up trash. Grace isn't speaking to anyone (no one knows why) but it doesn't seem so bad to me. And The Destructor is living in his cat box, talking all the time."

"So, pretty much everything is back to normal," Lonnie says.

"About as normal as Thomas Blackthorne lifting 27 pounds 8.96 ounces with his tongue," I say, "which I think we can agree is not normal at all."

Lonnie and Viva laugh at my joke, but really, I

don't feel funny. I feel like climbing into my tent and hiding out for a very long time.

ALONE IN THE AVIARY

Grumpy Pigeon Man woke me up this morning. But when I scramble over he's still in his pajamas and isn't looking so good. His nose is super red, and he's hacking up stuff from his lungs that looks about as old as he is. I take a step back.

"I'b god uh code," he says. His nose is clearly all stuffed up. "I'b go-ig bag to bed. Tage care ob dem dis abdernoon. I'll see you to-barro." He slowly shuffles away.

I can't believe it. He's leaving me to look after the birds. Without him. It only took like a month. I can't mess this up.

I do everything just the way he likes. The right amount of food. I don't spill any. I check Dad's watch, which I still have, so I'll know when ten minutes is up. I fill up the water dish. I clean their bath bowl and give them fresh bathwater, and take away the food when the time is up. I do it all just right, and Grumpy Pigeon Man is not even there to see me. Of course.

Instead of rushing back to my tent like I usually

do to get
ready for
school, I
turn over
the bucket
and sit down
like Grumpy
Pigeon Man
does.

I know it's
crazy that I'm sitting on
a bucket watching a bunch of pigeons, but they're
so interesting you forget you're sitting on a bucket
watching a bunch of pigeons.

Sitting like this is different from walking in
and feeding them. It's like looking into the dark
and at first you don't see anything, then slowly
your eyes get used to it and you see more and
more.

They peck, scratch, fluff, and coo like usual,
but then I notice that some are quiet and still.
Others flap. They even look at me. Honest to gosh
look at me. Like I'm somebody. I could sit here all
day except I've got to go to school.

Just as I stand up to leave a pigeon flaps down
and lands on my shoulder. I can't believe it. Right

on my shoulder. It coos in my ear. A sound so soft
it's like a pillow.

And then it poos. I can't believe it. Right on
my shoulder. I thought we were friends.

VIVA TAKES CHARGE

Lonnie and Viva are in my backyard. Viva really
knows how to take charge.

During lunch, I told them how Grumpy
Pigeon Man was sick and how I got to do everything without him. (I left out the part about the
pigeon pooing on me.) Viva jumped on this and
said how I'd always said he'd never let us come
over but that this was our once-in-a-lifetime
chance (her words). And before I could disagree
she called her mom from the office and asked if
she could come over after school and got Lonnie
to do the same.

So Mom didn't ask any questions when we all
showed up because Viva's mom had called her.
It was a similar call to Halloween but this time
she asked if my mom would be home the whole
time and what Viva would get for a snack, and
said what time she'd come to pick her up. I have a
feeling Viva's mom will be absolutely on time. I'm

pretty sure this is one of those differences Viva talks about.

"This is my tent," I say. Viva pokes her head in.

"Totally cool."

"And there are the pigeons." I point across the fence to their house.

The three of us walk a little closer.

"Let's go," she says.

"I don't know," I say. "If he catches us he'll go ballistic."

"Oh brother." Viva rolls her eyes. "If he's as sick as you say, he won't come out. He's bound to be tucked in bed fast asleep. That's what my grandpa does when he has a cold."

Lonnie shakes his head. "You haven't met the guy."

"So he yells a little. What's the big deal?" She opens the gate that goes out of our yard and into his. Lonnie and I follow, both of us wondering, Who put Viva in charge?

SNEAKING IN

"Boy, it's stinky," Viva says. She holds her nose.

"I've seen enough." Lonnie turns to go.

Viva grabs his arm. "Lonnie, it's just a smell.

It can't hurt you."

"It's not the smell I'm afraid of."

"Stop worrying," Viva says. "Oh look! Cubbies like in kindergarten."

"Those are nesting boxes," I explain. A few birds are cuddled in.

"What's in there?" Viva points to the loft.

"Come on, Viva," Lonnie says.

"Just one more minute, then we'll leave. I promise."

I lead them through the second door and out into the loft.

"How many does he have?" Viva asks.

"Fifty-seven."

"That's a lot of pigeons."

"I had to count them five different times."

"How do you tell them apart?"

"You get to know them," I say.

Lonnie looks torn. I know he doesn't want to get caught by Grumpy Pigeon Man, but the pigeons are cool. I understand his feelings. Maybe if I do my job, it'll take my mind off Grumpy Pigeon Man catching us.

I grab the feed and pour it in. I'm about to get water when Viva scoops up some of the feed and kneels down. She stays real still. A pigeon comes over and eats right out of her hand. Now why didn't I think of that? I reach into the food and pull some out and kneel down too. A pigeon comes over and eats out of my hand.

It tickles.

Lonnie does the same and the three of us stay there as the pigeons eat out of our hands.

"Did you know," I say real quiet, "there isn't a single record about pigeons in *The Guinness Book of World Records*?"

Out of nowhere The Destructor's scream cuts through the quiet. "TEDDDDDYYYYYY!

HEYYYY, TEDDDDDYYYYYY!"

The pigeons scatter onto their perches. Lonnie and Viva stand up, startled as much as the birds. "Oh no!" I say. "Let's get out of here."

MOST DANGEROUS PINNIPED

The Destructor is staring at us from over the fence. "I want to come in, too!" He's loud. "MOOOOOMMM! Teddy and his friends are with the pigeons. I WANT TO GO!"

Lonnie and Viva head for the door. I stay because I need to take away the pigeons' food and be sure everything is shut tight.

I hear that familiar door slam and look up just as Lonnie and Viva run smack into Grumpy Pigeon Man, who strangely is moving faster than usual and looks as dangerous as a leopard seal (the record holder for the most dangerous pinniped). It's not a pretty sight.

The only difference is that Grumpy Pigeon Man is not a pinniped (fin-footed mammal). But other than that he looks like he's going to eat us alive, which is exactly what a leopard seal would do.

LOUD AND CLEAR

There are all sorts of loud sounds in *The Guinness Book of World Records*: finger snap, scream, shout, snore, even tongue click, but my personal favorite is the burp.

The loudest burp ever recorded was by Paul Hunn. I have no idea what a decibel meter reading is, but he got to 109.9 of them. I know that it was louder than a pile driver heard from 100 feet (they say so in the book) so it must be loud, and clearly it was worthy enough for *The Guinness Book of World Records*.

Grumpy Pigeon Man must have come pretty close to that decibel level. I thought he'd never stop yelling at us, which proves why I was nervous about this whole thing, even if he was sick.

The three of us cowered. Mom came out, looking mad, and let Grumpy Pigeon Man holler at us that we had no right to go in there and not ask him, and that he hired me, not these two, and what if something happened to his pigeons while we were there? And all the time he was bellowing, The Destructor cooed at the pigeons from outside the aviary.

"I'm really sorry," Viva says, looking Grumpy Pigeon Man right in the face. "Teddy told us all about your pigeons, and we really wanted to meet them. What can we do to make it up?"

And it's like Grumpy Pigeon Man is under her Jedi Mind Trick, because I thought he was going to fire me but instead he says, "De abiary deeds a good clead-ig."

CLEANING CREW

Two days later, Lonnie and Viva are back at my house, pulling on our pink protective plastic gloves. Mom also bought us face masks. I don't know why but she is convinced we need them. Of course, The Destructor doesn't have to clean, even though he's the reason we're in this mess.

"I'm surprised your mom didn't put us in space suits," Lonnie says. "Actually I'm surprised my own mother didn't."

Viva whispers, "I didn't tell my mom."

"What?" Lonnie says. "You're crazy."

"I know," Viva says. "But when Mrs. Mars

didn't say anything to her I thought I wouldn't say anything either." She pauses. "You don't know how hard it is to be the only child. No one else does anything wrong."

We walk outside and head for the aviary.

"How long do you think it'll take?" Lonnie asks.

Viva says, "We'll be lucky if we're done by dinner."

"In *The Guinness Book of World Records* there is only one entry for fastest cleaning," I say. "And that's window cleaning—9.14 seconds. Maybe we could break a world record for fastest aviary cleaning."

"I'll pass on that record," Lonnie says.

"Too boring," Viva says.

"I actually agree. If I'm going to break a world record I want it to be good. Really good."

Grumpy Pigeon Man waits for us with brooms, scrapers, and buckets. He explains what to do, and then sits down on a bucket and gives orders the whole time.

When we're finally done it is time for dinner. Grumpy Pigeon Man examines our work and says, "Your friends can come again. But only with you, Tent Boy." And he walks away.

I can tell you, we didn't break a world record for cleaning, but when Grumpy Pigeon Man said that, I felt like we did.

"*Tent Boy?*" Lonnie and Viva blink at me.

"If you ever want back in the aviary, you'll forget you ever heard that name."

"What name?" they say together.

I EARNED IT!

Yes! I finally did it!

All the grumblings, all the early mornings, all the afternoons, all the grouching, then the cleaning, and I was sure he'd fire me, but he didn't. And it was all worth it!

Not including tax, the Coleman StormBeam Dynamo lantern cost $34.99 and it is mine.

I know I should have gotten an alarm clock but Grumpy Pigeon Man is my alarm clock and he doesn't seem to mind.

LAST NIGHT

Pants, shirt, socks, hat, pajamas, slippers, sweater, mittens, snow pants, parka, and I was still freezing cold! Fall is definitely over.

Now I really wish I had bought a sleeping bag.

FINALLY

I may be freezing cold but I love my lantern. I've been looking for a third pigeon fact for my report for so long. I finally got it: Tipplers are famous for endurance. They can fly for twenty-two hours and never stop!

You've got to admit, Ms. Raffeli, I've got endurance, too.

1. The Destructor is related to me.
2. I work for Grumpy Pigeon Man.
3. I didn't give up on finding a third fact. (Another third fact! HA!)

HOMEWORK: A POEM FOR THE ROLLERS AND TUMBLERS (PIGEONS)

Because everything takes so long to do in school, Ms. Raffeli is combining subjects. Since we're still studying birds and we're on our poetry unit, she's decided we should write poems that connect to our birds.

This is what I wrote:

> *Tipplers, rollers, tumblers too.*
> *Lots of pigeons, but what do they do?*
> *They fly, they somersault, they soar up high.*
> *They're the Olympians of the sky.*

I think it's a pretty good poem. Strange but true, I think pigeons doing flips is cooler than 842 people belly dancing, which made it into *The Guinness Book of World Records*. Sure, it's the most belly dancers at one time, but come on, flipping pigeons!

THANKSGIVING

One of my most favorite pages in *The Guinness Book of World Records* is called "Projectiles." The whole page is about different objects and how far they have been thrown. People will throw anything.

a watermelon seed spit: 75 feet 2 inches

 a cherry stone spit: 93 feet 6.5 inches

a cow pat: 226 feet

 a brick: 146 feet 1 inches

a rolling pin: 175 feet 5 inches

a 8.5 x 11–inch paper airplane: 207 feet 4 inches

There's also a raw egg that was thrown 323 feet 2 inches and caught without breaking!

I could go on but I think you see what I mean. They are all curiously ordinary things.

The Projectiles page reminds me of my family and Thanksgiving.

We go to Gran's for Thanksgiving. We drive there, arrive late (of course), eat lunch, and then are told not to stay and help with the cleanup.

For weeks after every Thanksgiving, we get packages from Gran containing the projectiles that we threw around her house: sweaters, sneakers, Frisbees, books, markers, cell phones. You name it; we've left it.

This year is no different. Except this year, we forgot to bring The Destructor's cat box home. Gran says she's not mailing that back, and that her cat started using it anyway.

Mom bought a new one for The Destructor even though she still hasn't bought me an alarm clock. I wonder how far I'd have to throw The Destructor and his cat box to get onto the Projectiles page?

DECEMBER

DETERMINATION

"It is too cold," Mom says. She's right. It is cold. "You will not sleep out there in this weather."

But one of the things you learn about from reading *The Guinness Book of World Records* is determination.

For example, Graham Hicks set records for fastest speeds on a quad bike and an aquabike, which is a fancy way of saying Jet Ski. Sure, that's amazing, but on top of that, he's deaf and blind. You know there were a lot of people out there saying he couldn't do it. Clearly, he did not listen to them. I'm not going to listen either. I'm staying in my tent.

I think.

DETERMINATION PART 2

It's Saturday night and I've already had dinner and brushed my teeth. Now I'm back in my tent, trying to stay warm and wondering why I bought the lantern to read by instead of a sleeping bag made for the arctic.

I'm not telling anyone how tempted I am to sleep inside. It's cold out here. Really cold. I'm not certain I have Graham Hicks's determination. I decide I'll go in for just a little bit. I'll get more clothes for next week, new comic books to read, and after my toes thaw, I'll come back out.

Dad putters in the kitchen. "Are you sleeping inside tonight?"

"No, just getting a few things." I hurry up the stairs before he tries to change my mind.

I admit, when I walk in my room I scream. I've only been away from it for eight hours but everything is destroyed.

My comics are all over the floor. My Star Wars figures are out of order, five of my Ewoks are missing their feet, and Chewbacca has completely disappeared.

"Okay, Destructor, where's Chewy?" I grab him by the arms. He howls.

Sharon rushes in from the bathroom where

she's been singing and disconnects us. "You're the one who moved out," she says.

"It's still my room."

"Not for much longer. Dad says if you keep living in the tent, he'll give it all to Jake."

I feel just like I did when I read about Ken Edwards, the guy who ate 36 cockroaches. But that guy had determination. And so do I. I'm determined that The Destructor won't ruin my life.

I grab all my important stuff: my comics, figures, my card collection. I find Chewy in the

closet, I find the Ewoks' feet under my bed, and I bring them to the tent. I don't feel the cold anymore. I remember why I live here. I'm safe from The Destructor.

I'M NOT COUNTING

"Hey, Teddy," Grace yells, unzipping my tent without my permission and standing outside with a hat, gloves, parka, and a scarf on. "You know you've been out here for sixty-six days?"

Grace must have no one else to annoy.

"No, Grace. And I'm not counting. Close the tent." Of course she doesn't.

"You are such a nut-o. I mean, really, you must want to sleep in the house. It's freezing cold out here. The house is so toasty and warm."

"I'm fine," I say, just as she takes my picture.

"I'll come back tomorrow to photograph you and the icicles hanging from your nose. If you're still alive."

GRUMPY PIGEON MAN'S SURPRISE

The next morning in the aviary, I have to chip away at a thin layer of ice in the pigeons' water

bowl. They get super fluttery
when I pour their feed in. I
figure the cold makes them
want to eat more. Grumpy
Pigeon Man still points
out every little thing I do wrong. Who could
do everything right with him staring over his
shoulder?

I'm about to leave when he says, "Hold it one
second, Tent Boy."

It's hard not to wonder if he will ever learn my
real name.

About ten minutes later he comes back carrying an orange bundle. He tosses it to me. "You
might need this tonight."

I can't believe it. He's given me a brand-new
sleeping bag. A really good one. I'm speechless.

He walks away and I'm left there wondering why he would do this.

And then, like he can hear the inside of my head, he turns around and shouts, "By the time you save up enough money for a sleeping bag you'll be dead from frostbite and I'll have to find someone else to take care of my pigeons. I'm too old for that." He slams his door.

I should have known the reason he doesn't want me to die is because of his pigeons.

FINAL PROJECT

Ms. Raffeli gave us our final bird project weeks ago. We're supposed to have been writing on what we've learned about our bird. I mean I like pigeons, but writing a report is so boring and now it's due tomorrow and I still don't have an idea.

I'm in the aviary. Grumpy Pigeon Man is checking my work.

"You seem distracted, Tent Boy."

I explain about the report and how I can't think of anything interesting.

"You can't find anything interesting about pigeons?"

I feel a little stupid when he says this, but I nod.

"I'll give you interesting." He pulls up two buckets. We sit. "It was World War I," he says. "A U.S. division was stuck behind enemy lines and in real danger. Not only was the enemy attacking, but the Allies didn't know the division was there and were also attacking."

"What are allies?"

"Ask your mother," he says and keeps talking. "They had to get a message to the Allies. But that was close to impossible because the only way to get a message was by pigeon."

"Why didn't they just phone?" I ask.

"No phones," he says. "No radios, no TVs, no computers, only pigeons."

"You mean they sent messages by pigeons?"

"You're smarter than you look, Tent Boy. They attached a message to the pigeon's legs and sent them off. Their homing instinct took care of the rest. They had three pigeons."

"Well, that's a lot," I say.

"It was, but the enemy fire was so intense that the birds had to fly up high or they would be shot down."

"What happened?"

"The first two birds didn't make it. They only had one left: Cher Ami."

"What does Cher Ami mean?" I ask.

I can tell he's about to say "go ask your mother" but instead says, "It's French for *dear friend*. Now stop interrupting. Where was I? Oh—so they attached the note and set him free. He flew up but was shot and dropped out of the sky."

"Then what?" I ask.

"All hope was gone."

"But Cher Ami was okay, wasn't he?"

"Hold your horses, I'm getting there. Out of nowhere, Cher Ami came flying up. He flew higher and higher until he was safe."

I admit my heart is pounding. "Then what?"

"That bird flew twenty-five miles in twenty-five minutes and reached the Allies. The Allies read the message and they rescued the division."

"What about Cher Ami?"

"He had been shot in the eye, in the chest, and in his leg, which was hanging on by a tendon. If that tendon had broken the message would have been lost. They operated on Cher Ami and he lived. His leg could not be saved, but they made him a fake one and he was even awarded a medal. You can see him stuffed and on display at the Smithsonian Institution."

This time, I thank Grumpy Pigeon Man right away and run home to start my report. If *The Guinness Book of World Records* had a hero bird category, Cher Ami would hold it forever.

ALL SHE SAYS

"Interesting, Teddy," Ms. Raffeli says when she hands back my paper. "Not exactly what I asked for, but interesting." Her roller-coaster eyebrows rise up again. I wish I knew what they meant.

We don't get grades at my school, but when I look at my report I got a check plus.

Lonnie and Viva always get check pluses but not me. So, this time the eyebrows must have meant something good.

NAMES

After school, Lonnie and Viva come over to the aviary.

"Do you think he names his birds?" Viva asks. It's the kind of question she asks: kind of weird, and kind of cool at the same time.

"No," Lonnie says. "Grumpy Pigeon Man does not name his birds."

"Is that a boy or a girl?" she asks. Again, kind of weird, kind of cool.

"I don't know," I say. "And I am not looking."

"I just wondered if you'd learned to tell them apart."

"I know that male pigeons coo more than females."

Lonnie says, "If I were to name a bird, that bird there would be Admiral Ackbar. He's cooing a lot and he looks tough."

Viva laughs. "How about that one?"

"Padmé Amidala, and the pigeon next to her is Sabé."

"Can one be Jar Jar Binks?" I ask.

"That skinny one with the long neck."

"Look." I point at a pigeon whose head is tilted, and it looks worried.

We all say at the same time, "C-3PO." We crack up.

A pigeon flaps off its perch, landing next to another bird. "Have you met Chewbacca and Han Solo?" Viva says.

I point to four pigeons calmly perched and looking like they know something we don't. "They're totally the Jedi Masters: Obi-Wan Kenobi, Stass Allie, Yoda, and Ima-Gun Di."

A bird swoops past Lonnie's head. "Remember Paploo, the Ewok who steals the speeder? There he goes."

"What about those three?" Viva asks.

"Princess Leia, Luke Skywalker, and Lando Calrissian," Lonnie says. All three pigeons look up when he says this.

"They know their names," Viva says. "How many more birds to go?"

"We are not naming fifty-seven birds!" Lonnie says. "I'm not that crazy."

SOMETHING'S WRONG

"You're late getting up this morning," Mom says. She and The Destructor are already awake and eating breakfast when I come into the house.

"Grump—" I stop myself. "Mr. Marney didn't wake me."

"Maybe he decided to sleep in," she says.

"Maybe he doesn't want to be my alarm clock anymore."

"Teddy, check on him after you feed the pigeons."

Lately Grumpy Pigeon Man wakes me up then goes back inside. When I'm done, he comes out and checks my work. But today he doesn't come out after I'm done, so I go to his house and knock.

I've never been inside his house. In fact, no one I know has been in his house. No answer. I knock again. I think about getting Mom but I open the door instead.

"Mr. Marney?" I call. No answer. His kitchen

is clean and, like the aviary, very quiet. "Mr. Marney?"

He should be here. He doesn't go anywhere. That's why he can always be so grumpy about my family. He's always around to see what we do wrong.

From the kitchen I can see into the living room. I walk in. There's only a TV, one chair, and a shelf with trophies lined up like pigeons on their perches.

They have golden birds on them. He's got about twenty of these. Pigeon Racing Championship trophies. So cool. And I see some medals. They look like army stuff. I'm not surprised this guy was in the army. It makes sense.

"Mr. Marney?" All this quiet gives me the creeps. I'm getting Mom. As I turn to walk out, I see something:

By the chair.

There he is.

A bundle on the floor.

HOSPITAL

The Destructor is under the bed, of course. Grumpy Pigeon Man sleeps. A beeping machine tells us he's okay. He has a needle in his arm giving him fluids. I know it's weird but I'm still worried about him.

Strange but true, *The Guinness Book of World Records* has an entry for the most valuable cracker (really, a cracker). It survived a trip to the South Pole in 1907 with Ernest Shackleton, a famous explorer.

You know that cracker is old and inedible but it's still valuable. For some reason that cracker reminds me of Grumpy Pigeon Man.

"He'll be home in a few days," Mom says. "He doesn't have any family, so he'll need our help." His eyes flutter a little.

"Mom, what would happen to his pigeons if Grumpy Pigeon Man—"

"Mr. Marney," she says.

"If Mr. Marney weren't around?"

"I don't know, but what would've happened to him if *you* weren't around?"

Grumpy Pigeon Man wakes suddenly and frowns. "Something wrong with the pigeons?"

"No," I say. "The pigeons are fine."

"Then what are you doing here, Tent Boy?"

The Destructor's head pops out from under the bed. "Tent Boy!"

Mom leans over. "Seems like you didn't eat, Tom." Who'd have thought Grumpy Pigeon Man

had a first name and that it was something normal like *Tom*?

"Tent Boy! Tent Boy! Tent Boy!" The
Destructor sings.

"Stop it," I say.

Of course Mom ignores The Destructor. "From
now on, we'll be looking in on you twice a day."

He waves her aside. "Don't need help."

"If you want Teddy, then you get the rest of us,
too. We'll be back in the morning to see you."

The Destructor slides out from

under the bed, cupping his hand in Mom's and singing down the hall. "Tent Boy! Tent Boy! Tent Boy!"

I wonder how long I've got until Grace hears this.

GIANT SQUID

Out of the blue my parents remember the alarm clock that I needed months ago. It figures the only time they decide to help me out with this job is now that Grumpy Pigeon Man is sick.

"He's been waking you up all these months," Mom says, as we leave the hospital. "That was fine. He hired you. He needed to wake you up. But everything is different now. Mr. Marney needs our help and that means we have to help you."

When she says, "We have to help you," she doesn't mean she's buying me an alarm clock, even though that's what I need.

She means she'll wake me up by yelling out her bedroom window.

I tell Lonnie and Viva what's going on.

Viva looks at Lonnie. "You said she'd wake Teddy the same day a giant squid was finally found in its natural environment."

Lonnie says, "I did say that. Do you think they found one today?"

"Strange but true," I say, "I am wondering the same thing."

THEY FOUND ONE

As I'm leaving for school the next day Mom calls out to me. She's reading the paper, of course. "Teddy! Listen to this! A new world record was broken." She reads, "The giant squid has finally been filmed in its natural habitat!"

Strange but true, I fell over right then and there.

"Are you all right?" she asks.

"I'm fine," I say. "Just in shock."

"Did you know the eyeball of the giant squid is as big as a human head?"

I shake my head. The eyeball is weird, but really, the fact that they filmed a squid is weirder.

FAMILY DINNER

We're all at the table, but Caitlin and Casey are the only ones doing the talking. It's their last week of collecting trash but they still have a lot to say about it.

"We collected three barrels from the school grounds this morning," Caitlin says.

"Could we talk about something else?" Sharon asks.

"It seems like you two learned from this." Dad smiles.

"Definitely," Caitlin says. "For one thing everyone makes trash."

"For another thing," Casey says, "everyone wants their trash picked up."

"So we're starting a business," Caitlin says, "collecting trash on bikes."

"Because we can't drive yet," Casey adds.

Then they say together, "We're calling it: Trash Trikes."

Everything gets quiet. It hasn't been this quiet since I showed them the picture of Tom Leppard, the most tattooed senior citizen. The guy is completely covered in leopard-spot tattoos. And I do mean *completely* covered. On top of that, he's old, which is cool because it shows that old people can break records, but like I said, it really silences a crowd.

FAMILY DINNER PART 2

Silence never lasts long in my family.

"I think it's great," Mom says. "You're helping the planet and making money."

Sharon throws down her napkin. "Besides me, is there no one normal in this family?"

"What's that supposed to mean?" Maggie asks.

"Your running is a little over the top," Sharon says.

"You sing all the time," I say.

"That's normal," she says.

"Not the way you do it," Grace snorts.

Of course, instead of getting mad at Grace,

Sharon's eyes get all small at me. "At least I don't try breaking a world record every five minutes, obsess over pigeons, and, if you haven't noticed, live in a tent."

The Destructor, who is eating, as usual, in his cat box under the table, chooses that moment to shout, "Tent Boy! Tent Boy! Tent Boy!"

"Zip it," I say and kick him.

"Teddy, don't kick Jake. Jake, don't call your brother Tent Boy," Dad says.

"Tent Boy?" Grace's eyes light up. "Why didn't I think of that?"

"Because," The Destructor hollers, "Grumpy

Pigeon Man did!"

Mom says, "Jake, his name is Mr. Marney." But she looks straight at me.

"Tent Boy," Grace giggles between bites of food.

Sharon throws down her napkin. "Our family is nuts!"

I bury my head in my hand. Stupid Destructor, now I'll be Tent Boy forever!

WINTER HOLIDAYS

During math, Ms. Raffeli wants us to show all the ways we know how to make the number 2,312.

It is not going well. There is a buzz in the classroom that reminds me of what it must have sounded like when the magicians Penn and Teller magically made appear the most living creatures in a magic performance: 80,000 bees on TV.

It's possible that was louder but not by much. No one can focus on anything because of the holidays coming up.

Ms. Raffeli finally puts us out of our misery and brings us together on the rug.

"All right," she says, her eyebrows shooting up. "It's going to be a long month if we don't get this out of the way. I don't normally talk about religion or religious celebrations in the class but I find the month of December especially tiring if we don't." She grabs her marker and writes on chart paper. "The best-known celebrations in our country are Hanukkah, Christmas, and Kwanzaa, but there are other holidays too. For Buddhists it's Bodhi Day, and for pagans it's the Yule, which is celebrated on the winter solstice. Depending on their calendars, Muslims sometimes celebrate Eid al-Adha and Hindus celebrate Diwali." She writes all of these names on the paper.

"In this classroom, we have students who celebrate almost all of these holidays. Each one is wonderful and important. I want you to come up one by one and write your name next to the holiday your family celebrates."

We go up and put our names next to where they belong. And Ms. Raffeli is right. Nearly every single holiday gets filled up.

Viva writes her name in two places. Hanukkah and Christmas. She shrugs and says, "My mom is Jewish and my dad is Christian."

"You are so lucky," I say. And I really think she is. She's an only child and she gets two holidays.

WINTER IN THE TENT

We had our first big storm. Two feet of snow packed around the tent. Inside it's dry and once I slide in my sleeping bag I'm warm.

The hardest part is climbing out of my sleeping bag and into my boots. In *The Guinness Book of World Records* they say the coldest inhabited place on Earth is Oymyakon, Siberia, in Russia, at −90 degrees Fahrenheit. They must live in sleeping bags.

As I lie there, I can't help thinking about the olden days and how people got along without indoor plumbing. The problem with school is that they never answer the questions we want answered, like where did they go to the bathroom when it was below freezing? How did they go to the bathroom when it was so cold? And really, what did they use for toilet paper? When I ask Ms. Raffeli she does the tallest roller-coaster thing with her eyebrows.

Clearly, she doesn't know the answers either.

THE WEIRDNESS OF LONNIE'S BROTHER

After our family dinner last night, I feel like taking a break from them so I persuade Lonnie to go to his house after school even though it's a longer walk in the cold and Jerome is probably home.

"I'd rather deal with the wrath of your brother."

Lonnie agrees but only because something strange is going on with Jerome. "He's not around much. And he's distracted. He's not beating me up."

As it happens he is at home when we get there. I prepare for a punch to my arm, his usual greeting. But instead he says, "Hey, Teddy. How are you doing?"

I don't know what to say back. I'm still clenched tight waiting for the punch.

"How's your family?" he asks.

Now I'm really confused but somehow mumble, "Crazy as ever."

"Crazy as ever," he repeats and laughs like I made some sort of joke. "I'll see you both later." And he walks out of the room.

"That was weird," I say.

Lonnie shakes his head. "You can say that again."

MORE WEIRDNESS

"Weird," Viva says.

"Weird," I say.

"Weird," Lonnie says. The pigeons coo as if they agree with us.

We're sitting on buckets in the aviary. "I know I should be happy, but Jerome is acting crazy."

"I'd be careful," I say.

"Jerome stays late at school, says he has stuff to do, but never says what it is."

"What do your parents think?" Viva asks.

"Whatever they think they're not telling me. They keep saying I should be happy that Jerome has found something constructive to do and to let him have his privacy."

"So weird," Viva says.

"So weird," I say.

"So weird," Lonnie says.

Paploo flies down, landing at our feet and bobbing his head in agreement.

AND NOW GRUMPY PIGEON MAN IS ACTING WEIRD

Grumpy Pigeon Man seems healthy but he's acting as weird as Jerome. He hasn't come out to visit his birds once since getting home from the hospital.

Every day I knock on his door. "Not ready," he says, or "Too tired," or "No," and just in case I didn't read him loud and clear, he slams his door.

Mom cooks meals for him and Grace brings them over. At first, Grace refused but Mom said if she wanted to avoid ending up in a tent like me she'd do it. Grace agreed.

Pigeons are very social and even recognize people. I read that in the book from the library.

Of course, they know Grumpy Pigeon Man, and they must miss him, which is surprising since he's so grumpy. I guess pigeons don't care about grumpiness. But I can't figure out why he won't come. It makes no  sense. These birds are what he loves the most; you'd think he'd want to see them. Or at least be sure I'm still doing my job right.

And then, I wonder why I care. Why would I want him back? It's a lot more peaceful without him grouching at me.

Strange but true, Grumpy Pigeon Man not visiting his pigeons is weirder than Donald Gorske, who ate 20,500 Big Macs by the time he was thirty-three years old.

That's a lot of hamburgers. He must have loved hamburgers, but I know Grumpy Pigeon Man loves his birds more.

OUT OF IDEAS

All this weirdness and cold has slowed down my record breaking. I can't even think of a good one to try. Maybe I'll never get in that book.

That thought weighs me down just like how David Huxley must have felt pulling a Boeing 747-400 plane 298.5 feet in 1 minute 27.7 seconds. Totally by himself.

Why can't I do something like that?

CHRISTMAS TRADITION

Some people think that with so many kids in my family, Christmas must be huge and fantastic. They think I must get a pile of presents. Nothing is further from the truth. In my family, we draw one name out of a hat and give that person a present. My parents give each of us one additional present.

I got Grace this year. I was thinking of giving her padded shoes so when she slams on my feet it wouldn't hurt as much, but I couldn't find anything like that.

Grace opens the present I gave her. It's a book on photography. I think she actually likes it.

"Thanks, Tent Boy," she says.

I flinch. The present I really want is for her to stop calling me that. As soon as I find my present I know it's not from her and I don't have to wonder who it is from. The wrapping says it all. There's only one kid who would use a whole roll of Scotch tape. When I finally get to the bottom of it he's given me five boxes of paper clips.

"Thanks," I say. I don't sound enthusiastic.

"Tell Teddy why you gave him paper clips," Mom says. She looks real excited.

"So you can beat the world record!" Jake crows.

"He wants you to break a world record," she repeats.

"The only paper clip record is a chain that stretched for 22.25 *miles*. I'm going to need a lot more to break that record."

Christmas is saved slightly by my parents, who give me an alarm clock. Now that, I needed.

CHRISTMAS TRADITION PART 2

It's our year to have Christmas dinner at our house. By the time all of my relatives arrive, we'll be forty-three people.

On top of that, Mom invited Viva and her mom and dad because this is their first year here

and they don't have any family. Lonnie's away in Florida or his family would be here, too.

"I can't believe you invited Viva's family." I think this idea is about as good as being the fastest person to push an orange for one mile with your nose. (You *know* I don't think that's a good idea.) "Her parents will never let her come here again. I'm not even certain *she'll* ever want to come here again."

"They're going to love it!" Mom says, beating potatoes into mash. "And it's good timing. They leave tomorrow for a big ski trip. I invited Mr. Marney but he said he had plans."

"Of course he said that, Mom. Really? Who would want to be here?"

"What a terrible thing to say, Teddy." She hands me the bowl. "Here, beat these potatoes." She goes to the stove and lifts the lid on every pot, then slams them down. "We have a lovely family. I don't want to hear any more of this."

I hate to admit it but I kind of wish Grumpy Pigeon Man had agreed to come to dinner. I know he's lying about having plans. Where would he go? He doesn't have anyone else but us. And if he came over maybe I could stop thinking about how he hasn't visited his pigeons.

That's when the doorbell rings. "Here we go," I say. "Welcome to the circus." That's what Gran says whenever she sees us.

Mom gives me a hard stare. "I thought I made myself clear."

Viva and her mom and dad are the first to arrive. It must seem so normal right now, just our family and theirs. I think maybe I should warn them, but Viva rushes over to me and pulls out a video camera before I can say anything. "Look what I got, Teddy!"

"Wow," I say. And I mean it.

"How about you? What did you get?"

"You really don't want to know." The doorbell rings again, a nice excuse to get away. An alarm clock and five packages of paper clips seem pretty ridiculous compared to a video camera. And then I realize that I'm not really saved, because when I open the door the madness truly begins.

A swarm of relatives swooshes in. Coats and scarves are tossed into my arms. Hugs and kisses are planted on me without a question. I look over at Viva and her family. They look like deer in headlights. Frozen and about to be run over.

"I'm going to practice," Sharon says and heads up to her bathroom.

Whatever Dad thought about muffling the sound of her singing does not seem to be working tonight. It's clear as a bell. Aunt Irma suggests that maybe Sharon has practiced enough and someone should tell her. No one volunteers so Aunt Irma finally goes, and the singing stops for a few minutes until Aunt Irma's voice is heard singing with Sharon.

Some great-uncle whose name I can't remember starts talking to the twins. "I can never tell you two apart." He laughs, then says, "Help me out."

"I'm Caitlin," says Casey.

"And I'm Casey," says Caitlin.

Dad leaps over, interrupting their conversation, and threatens to extend their trash duty if they keep up their antics.

Viva's parents look a little bit better once the food comes out. They don't even seem to mind that there isn't anywhere for them to sit by the time they get through the buffet line, so they have to eat standing up.

But when Maggie demonstrates some soccer kick for a cousin and the ball flies past Viva's dad's face, startling him so he bumps into her mom and she spills her food all over him, they go back to looking unhappy.

And then Grace comes over and I think the trouble might really start. She's got her phone with her and is showing all the pictures she's taken over the last three months of my tent and me, and then telling everyone my nickname is *Tent Boy*, which they think is hilarious and they all start saying it.

I'd like to kick her in the shins but I think of Lonnie and his Jedi training and stop myself. I also think if I do that I'll only pay later.

Viva is very quiet. As quiet as she used to be when she first sat at Lonnie's and my lunch table. I'm wondering what she's thinking just as the real Christmas tradition begins.

CHRISTMAS TRADITION PART 3

Strange but true, one of the only mass participation records (the fancy way of saying a bunch of people doing something at the same time) I like is when 5,983 people sat on whoopee cushions. That's a lot of people making farting noises at one time. Luckily, it was only the sound.

One thing I've learned about grown-ups is that after a big meal, they all fart. Obviously twenty-seven adults farting is not as many as 5,983, but in my family it's not just the sound; it's the smell.

Granddad is the worst. He can clear a room with his stench. Really.

It's difficult to imagine that Viva's family is

prepared for the farting marathon. But by the look on Viva's and her parents' faces you wouldn't know it's happening. They ignore the whole thing. How they can possibly pull that off is unfathomable.

And of course, Jake is in his cat box the whole night. I admit, I finally lose it when he starts telling everyone about Mr. Marney's pigeons, about rollers and tumblers, about when to feed them and how much, about giving them baths, and everyone thinks he's so cute, especially when he curls up in his cat box and coos like he's a pigeon in one of the nesting boxes. The pigeons are *my* job. Not his.

It makes me want to puke!

Finally, everyone starts leaving, but to ruin things even more, it turns out The Destructor has a present for everyone who came. He's made a million little birdfeeders.

"He's been working on these for weeks," Mom says as she hands one to each family. "He found the pinecones, then covered them with peanut butter and birdseed."

The way she talks you'd think he'd broken a world record.

LONESOME GEORGE

At lunch Lonnie and Viva talk about their vacations.

"Your family is fantastic," Viva says. "Getting the camera and Christmas dinner were the best parts of the holiday."

"You didn't look like you were having fun."

"It's just so different from what we're used to."

"Was there the usual stupendous display of farting?" Lonnie asks.

"It was stupendous." Viva laughs.

"It's not that funny," I say.

Lonnie visited his aunt and uncle and cousins down in Florida. They went swimming, got to go to Disney World, and Lonnie was given three flying lessons. Really. This summer, he's going to learn to fly a plane.

I tell them about Mom inviting Grumpy Pigeon Man to Christmas dinner and how he said he couldn't make it but how when I headed out to my tent his light was on. I knew he was home alone on Christmas. And then I tell them how he still hasn't come out to see his pigeons.

"I'm worried," I say. "He's turning into Lonesome George."

"Who's Lonesome George?" Viva asks. "I don't know that record."

"The loneliest creature in *The Guinness Book of World Records*, the last tortoise of his species."

"Are you sure he's lonely?" Lonnie says. "Or is he just acting like Grumpy Pigeon Man?"

"That's just it, he's not acting like Grumpy Pigeon Man. Even when he was grumpy, he took care of his pigeons. Something is wrong, and I've got to figure it out."

MOST DANGEROUS ANT

A week after Christmas, the house is cleaned of decorations and we're back to school. Mom is in

the kitchen reading the newspaper when I walk in.
She doesn't stop reading. She just reaches behind
her and grabs a plate with cookies on it and a glass
of milk.

"Mom?"

"Hmmm?"

"Do you think Grumpy Pigeon Man—"

"Mr. Marney, Teddy."

Grace walks in. She stomps on my foot.

"Ouch!"

"Oh sorry, Tent Boy," she says and takes a
cookie from the plate and downs my milk.

I decide to ignore her. I have more important things on my mind than a dumb sister. "Mom, Mr. Marney hasn't come to see his pigeons. He got out of the hospital weeks ago."

"Are you worried he's still sick?"

"I don't know," I say. "I don't even know why I want the guy back."

"It's obvious," Grace says. "You want him back because you're a sucker for punishment, and he doesn't want to go to his birds because when he got sick it scared him so much that he doesn't want to be close to them."

Grace offering good advice about people is about as likely as surviving the world's most dangerous ant bite. This ant is not like the small ones that eat our garbage. This ant has a poison that can kill a grown-up in fifteen minutes. Need I say more?

Mom nods. "I think Grace is right."

"Right about what?"

"It's strange grown-up stuff called psychology," Grace says like she's a million years older than me. "I read about it in one of Mom's magazines. They push away the things that are most important to them, so they never have to lose them."

"You mean he loves them so much he's afraid of them?" I ask.

"Exactly."

"So what do I do?" I ask her.

"What am I, a fortune-teller?" She stalks out of the room.

I look at my mom for help. She's back to her newspaper.

Clearly, I'm on my own here.

Now I'm wondering, is it smart to take advice from the world's most dangerous ant?

GETTING HIM

The thought of bringing Grumpy Pigeon Man and his pigeons together sticks to me like the world's stickiest salamander. Its skin is so sticky that when an animal bites it, the animal's mouth gets glued shut.

Viva, Lonnie, and I are in the loft with the pigeons and a pile of books about pigeons.

"I thought we were done with our bird unit," Viva says.

"Less talking, more reading," I say.

"Did you know pigeons and doves are related?" Viva asks.

"Pigeons bob their heads to see better," Lonnie says. "It helps with their depth perception."

"Cool," Viva says.

"It's cool but it's not helping," I say.

"What are you hoping to find?" Lonnie asks.

"I don't know," I say. "I just feel like if Suresh Joachim Arulanantham can stand on one foot for 76 hours and 40 minutes, I can find something that will get Grumpy Pigeon Man to visit his birds."

MAYBE

It's while I'm running back to my tent that I get my idea. I can't believe I didn't think of it before. Maybe forgetting to use the bathroom before going to bed helped me.

Maybe running in the freezing cold helped me.

Maybe I under-stand why Maggie loves to run so much.

Maybe it would help me think of a new world record to break.

Maybe I should get into my sleeping bag before I die of frostbite.

GOT HIM

The next morning I go straight to Grumpy Pigeon Man's back door. I knock.

When he opens the door I say, "Mr. Marney, all I'm going to say is: Cher Ami."

"Cher Ami to you, too," he says.

"I mean the pigeon."

"The pigeon?"

"The pigeon."

"Try to make a little sense, Tent Boy."

"Cher Ami," I say again.

"And your point is?"

"Your pigeons need you just like that division needed Cher Ami."

Grumpy Pigeon Man is quiet, then says, "It's a point. I just don't know if it's a good one."

STAY STILL

The pigeons look over and coo hello when I come feed them later that day. After all this time, they definitely know me.

I turn over a bucket and sit down. Paploo sits quietly next to me. I put some feed in my hand and he eats out of it. My plan did not work. Grumpy Pigeon Man doesn't come out. I really thought Cher Ami would get him. I wonder if he'll sell his pigeons. Why have them, if he doesn't like them?

That's when I see his door open. He walks to the aviary and comes inside. I can't believe it. My idea worked. I feel this huge smile growing on my face.

In my old copy of *The Guinness Book of World Records* there is a list of the longest bridges in the world. There's a record for each kind of bridge: cable suspension bridge, cantilever bridge, concrete girder bridge, floating bridge, steel arch bridge, wooden bridge, road and rail bridge system, and plain, old bridge.

My grin is definitely as long as the longest plain, old, regular bridge, the Second Lake Pontchartrain Bridge (23.87 miles). I can't help it. I got him to come out.

He pulls over a bucket. "What are you doing?"

"Feeding Paploo," I say. I'm so excited he's out here I forget that I never told him about naming the pigeons.

"Paploo? What's a Paploo?"

"It's an Ewok, sir."

"Tent Boy, that is not an Ewok."

"No, I mean it's named after an Ewok."

"You named my pigeons?"

"Not all of them. You have too many. And I didn't name them by myself, Lonnie and Viva helped."

Princess Leia flies down and sits on his knee. He pets her.

"That's so cool. I want a bird to do that to me. One time one of your birds flew onto my shoulder, but never my leg."

"You need to stay quiet," he says. "Do you

think you can do that?"

It's hard. My body jerks and wants to move around.

"Stay still," he repeats. "You can do it." And just like that, Obi-Wan Kenobi flies over. He almost lands on my knee, but then I squirm and he flaps away.

"Then again, maybe you can't."

"Obi-Wan Kenobi, come back," I say.

Grumpy Pigeon Man points to the bird on his leg. "Who's this?"

"Princess Leia."

"You named every pigeon after Star Wars?"

I'm impressed he even knows what Star Wars is. "Not all fifty-seven," I say, and then tell him the names we did come up with.

Grumpy Pigeon Man shakes his head. "I never thought they'd be named after Star Wars."

We sit there together staring at Obi-Wan Kenobi. And we never mention Cher Ami.

112 DAYS IN THE TENT

"You're such a nut-o, Tent Boy," Grace says. CLICK! STOMP!

Need I say more?

OF COURSE

Grumpy Pigeon Man is back to normal and tells me everything I do wrong, which seems right. The only difference now is he only comes out in the afternoon. "You can handle the mornings yourself," he says. "And you finally got an alarm clock."

He watches me bustle around feeding the birds, but after I'm done we always sit. I'm getting better at staying still.

And then it happens. Jar Jar Binks lands on my knee.

I'm so amazed that for a second I can't speak and when I finally do the words come out all quiet. "I did it."

"Of course you did, Tent Boy."

He says this like I'm the only one who believed I couldn't.

POSSIBLE REASONS

Lonnie, Viva, and I sit with the pigeons. We each have one on our knee. We're making a list of the possible reasons Jerome might be acting so strange. Last night, he gave Lonnie his baseball card collection.

"If that's not weird I don't know what is," Lonnie says.

"What about a girlfriend?" Viva suggests.

"Girlfriend?" we say together. "Who would date him?"

Alien brain invasion is at the top of our list.

THE KIND OF MOM SHE IS

Sharon sings continually and asks Mom how she sounds almost every second. She also makes Mom rehearse all her dumb lines for the play while Mom cooks dinner. Mom does it because that's the kind of mom she is.

Caitlin and Casey are building an extension for their bikes so they can haul trash. Mom helps them because that's the kind of mom she is.

Soccer training has started again for Maggie. She wasn't sure she was going to make the team again after The Destructor's stunt, but Mom went and talked to the coach. Mom can be very convincing. She said it wasn't right to exclude Maggie, and finally the coach agreed. That's the kind of mom she is.

Grace is always private about what she does. She whispers a lot to Mom and Mom whispers back so no one can hear them, because that's the kind of mom she is.

And for a little while, life seemed normal. But then The Destructor had to ruin it.

Yesterday, Aunt Ellen sent me a present after she visited the Guinness World Records Museum in Niagara Falls, Canada. It was an official Guinness World Records shirt and this particular one was autographed by Ashrita Furman, who pogo-sticked 23.11 miles.

Unbelievably, today The Destructor snuck into my tent and took the shirt. He also snuck into Mom's makeup bag. I was walking into the house after school when he hopped downstairs. His face, neck, arms, hands, and my entire shirt were covered in nail polish, eye makeup, and lipstick. Mom didn't get mad at all. She laughed and said she couldn't believe how cute he looked and took pictures. Unfortunately, that's also the kind of mom she is.

And once again The Destructor is prohibited

from entering my tent because that's the kind of brother he is.

RECORD ATTEMPT 9

Last night a huge snowstorm came through. We had more than three feet of snow, which was when I got the inspiration to break a new record.

Tallest snow mound.

FAILED ATTEMPT 9

I'm telling you it was tall. I worked for the whole weekend. It reached up to the second story windows. At least it did until I went to school on Monday, because when I came home The Destructor had burrowed a hole through the middle and caused an avalanche.

Now it looks like a plate of mashed potatoes.

I am never talking to that kid again.

FEBRUARY

BIRTHDAYS

No one believes me when I tell them, but it's true. Every single person in my family, except me, has a birthday in February.

February 1: Dad
February 5: Sharon
February 7: Maggie
February 10: Caitlin and Casey
February 14: Mom
February 15: Grace
February 20: THE DESTRUCTOR

In 1900 Johann Hurlinger walked the longest

distance on his hands (870 miles). Like the feats of the tippler pigeon, that takes endurance. If you live in my family, so does the month of February.

BIRTHDAY #1: DAD

Dad likes bowling on his birthday. Every year we go bowling. Usually, I have a good time bowling, even with The Destructor. Last year I helped him get a strike. I stood with him, guided his hand, and told him when to let go. When the last pin fell, he hugged me tight and said that it was all because of me. This year, Maggie and I bowl as a team and in a different lane from The Destructor.

He bowls with Grace and spends most of his time throwing his balls into other lanes, ruining the games of the people around us. Grace thinks this is hilarious, but the bowling alley owners finally move us to the lanes on the very end where no one is next to us.

Dad is happy because they give us free pizza and coupons for free bowling, and we get to start all over again.

The Destructor keeps asking me to bowl with him. "I haven't gotten a strike," he says.

"Oh well," I say. "I don't have a record for the

tallest snow mound or a clean T-shirt, and do you see me complaining?"

I'm just about to bowl a strike. The ball is perfectly poised for success when it is knocked into the gutter by another ball. I don't have to look over to know what happened.

It's got The Destructor written all over it.

BIRTHDAY #2: SHARON

"All I want for my birthday is to see a musical," Sharon says.

"We can do that," Dad says.

Sharon's eyes light up. "Really? You'll take me to the theater?"

"No, no," Dad says. "I mean we'll watch one at home."

Sharon scowls. "That is not what I meant."

"Do you know how much it costs to see a musical?"

"Never mind," she says. "I'll go out with friends."

From my tent, I hear the sounds of the TV. Mom and Dad are watching the musical with The Destructor. They seem to be having fun. I can even hear them singing along.

If I were Sharon I'd go out with friends too.

BIRTHDAY #3: MAGGIE

Maggie chose rock climbing. Unlike seeing a musical, this is something the whole family can do together. She and Grace have already been up and down about twenty times. Sharon had rehearsal and the twins passed on this because they need to map out their trash collecting route.

Mom was not thrilled. She likes us to be together for every birthday, but because Maggie doesn't care, Mom couldn't make a fuss.

I think they're crazy. This is the best birthday ever.

I'm almost to the top when The Destructor swings into me and grabs the hold I was reaching for. He steps on my foot, pushes off, and gets to the top first.

Everyone claps for him.

When we come back down the guy who works there says, "I've never seen a kid go up so fast." He hands The Destructor a lollipop.

This seems about as amazing as the largest gathering of Elvis impersonators (645). I mean, fine. Elvis was an amazing musician, or at least my gran tells me he was, but really, so what?

It's the same with The Destructor. He's fast, but giving him credit for it misses the whole point that he cheated to get what he wanted.

Nothing personal, but I would not want to get into *The Guinness Book of World Records* as an Elvis impersonator and I would not like to be the fastest kid to climb a rock wall if it meant I cheated.

BIRTHDAY #4: THE TWINS

The twins decide that for their birthday we will all bike. They have wagons attached to the back of their bikes ready to collect trash with the name of their business painted on the side.

Sharon does not come along. "I have a rehearsal," she says.

I try to get out of it, too, but Mom ignores me. Obviously, she knows Sharon is too old to boss around but I'm ten so I don't have a choice.

Have you ever tried to bike with eight people? It's not fun.

The Destructor rides on a Tag Along with Dad. You would think this would keep him safe but he's figured out how to make it swing side to side so he blocks anyone from passing him. By anyone, I mean me.

It is a long boring day except for dessert. The twins don't like cake so we make ice cream sundaes, and when The Destructor's not looking I eat half of his.

BIRTHDAY #5: MOM

Mom decides to go out with just Dad. This means we all have to stay home together.

"Be good," Mom says at the door. "And be sure to help each other out. We won't be home late." They leave looking a little too happy.

Maggie ties her shoelaces. "I'm going for a run before dark."

Grace is chasing the twins around because they've hidden the remote control.

Sharon rolls her eyes. "I'm going to my room," she says and leaves.

"More spaghetti," The Destructor says, handing me his plate from inside the cat box.

"They had better bring me back some cake," I say as I scoop spaghetti.

BIRTHDAY #6: GRACE

They didn't bring me cake and Grace's birthday is the next day. Grace's idea of a good party is to watch a scary movie and then sneak out in the middle of the night, shine a light in my face, and scream at the top of her lungs.

"I don't know why you're so mad," she says to Mom. "Teddy is fine. It was my birthday and it didn't cost anything."

BIRTHDAY #7: THE DESTRUCTOR

"I'll be in the pigeon coop today," I say.

"You won't," Mom says. "You know what day it is. You will be with us at the indoor water park."

"All of us?" I ask. "That's expensive for a birthday."

Mom shakes her head. "No, just you, Jake, Dad, and me."

"Mom, that's not fair. I don't want to spend the day with The Destructor."

"Fair or not, it's what Jake wants."

And that's why instead of a quiet day with the pigeons I am bombarded by a just-turned-five-year-old at the water park while my parents sit on the side and watch.

"Oh, Teddy, Jake's so happy," Mom calls, smiling her head off, just as he explodes out of the slide and crashes into me.

143 DAYS IN TENT

It's been a long month of birthdays but this doesn't stop Grace.

"I don't care how many times I do this, Tent Boy, it's still hilarious."

CLICK!

AFTER THE HAZE

I wish I could think of a record to break, but after all those birthdays my brain is as fried as the largest fried chicken meal (2,372 pounds 2.72 ounces).

SOMETHING IS WRONG

Even from the back door, I can tell right away something's wrong. The tent tilts to one side, and the zipper is half-open. It wasn't like that when I left this morning for school.

I run out to check on it. My sleeping bag is smooshed in one corner, my clothes are scattered, and my action figures are thrown everywhere, instead of in their straight lines. And there's a bag of microwave popcorn on the floor that's moving.

I wonder where it came from since I didn't eat any popcorn, but I *really* wonder why it's moving. Popcorn bags don't move on their own. I back away.

That's when I see it: the stripe of white. The universal warning sign. I let out a yelp and stumble backward, trying to get away. I drag myself as far away as I can. But I'm not fast enough. The skunk whose head is stuck in the bag of popcorn senses danger.

"Please don't," I whisper and run back to the house screaming.

I must have been screaming pretty loud because Mom and The Destructor rush toward me and then stop suddenly and gag.

"Oh my," Mom says.

The Destructor holds his nose. "Blech!" he says.

Mom says, "Don't come in."

"I almost got skunked and you're not letting me in?"

"Oh, honey," she says. "You *were* skunked."

I stand on the steps and watch as the skunk pulls free of the popcorn bag and trundles off into the woods behind our house.

CLEANUP

"Teddy! Your bath is ready," Mom calls me. I'm staying home from school today. This was agreed between Principal Johnson, Ms. Raffeli, and my parents. Clearly, we all think it's an excellent idea.

Dad gulps down his coffee and gives me a thumbs-up on his way out the door. "I'd hug you, kiddo, but I'm going to work."

I don't take it personally; I wouldn't hug a skunk if I had to go to work either.

DAY OFF

There are three things I've learned through this ordeal.

1. When skunks have babies they come out during the day and stay in their dens at night (to protect the babies).
2. Soaking in tomato baths is supposed to get rid of skunk smell.
3. I'm pretty sure it does nothing, except now I smell like skunk *and* tomatoes.

This was not the kind of day off I imagined.

DAY OFF: DAY 2

As I sink down into another tomato juice bath I picture The Destructor's punishment. Maybe he should live in the basement for two weeks, or eat only slugs, or walk the Great Wall of China, the longest wall in the world (2,150 miles). BAREFOOT.

Strange but true, my parents are not asking for my opinion about possible punishments for The Destructor. My parents won't hear of it. They say he's too young and won't understand.

"He's five," I yell to Mom as I get dressed. My fingers are pruney and I'm all red. "He's old enough to know he's not allowed in my tent! And he snuck in when no one was looking." I stop talking and do that tall eyebrow thing that Ms. Raffeli does so Mom understands that I'm serious. "He played with all my things, brought food into the tent, and left it unzipped."

"I hate to say this, Teddy," Mom says. "But if you let him in once in a while, then he wouldn't have to sneak in."

"AAAAAGH!" I scream and stalk off to the pigeons. The only place I can go.

DAY OFF: DAY 3

I'm still sleeping in the tent. No way am I sleeping in the house. Every morning I take the tent down.

Mom washes it and dries it, then I set it up again. No matter how much she washes it, it still stinks. Just like me, and my sleeping bag, which I am not using; the smell is too much even for me. Luckily the weather is warm enough so I don't need it.

I'm still taking care of the birds because, as Grumpy Pigeon Man says, "They're not bothered by skunk smell." Although obviously he is because he takes a step backward every time I come over to feed them.

"You're a lot faster setting up that tent," Grumpy Pigeon Man says.

"Under two minutes," I say.

"Still can't get rid of the smell?"

"Nope," I say. "And if I have one more tomato bath, I'll probably turn into one."

DAY OFF: DAY 4

Mom decides to give me a bath break. My skin is looking so strangely red that she's worried.

The doorbell rings, and Mom answers it.

"Teddy, it's Mr. Marney," she calls.

He follows her into the kitchen and then hands her a bottle. "Tomato juice won't work. This is my own mixture. Give Tent Boy a good soak in it. It'll get the smell off."

Notice how Grumpy Pigeon Man is allowed to call me Tent Boy and Mom doesn't correct him.

"Can I use it on the tent and sleeping bag?"

Grumpy Pigeon Man nods and sits down.

He picks up my copy of *The Guinness Book of World Records*. "Haven't seen one of these for years. Used to love it."

"You know it?" I ask.

"I may be old but I'm not a dinosaur." He flips through it. "Still nothing about pigeons. You'd think at least Cher Ami would be in there." He sighs and stands up.

"Thanks, Mr. Marney." Mom shows him to the door, then says, "Time for another bath. Hopefully this will do the trick."

Strange but true, I should be excited about a tomato-free bath, but all I can think about is what Grumpy Pigeon Man just said.

I know there isn't a single pigeon record, but for some reason thinking about it this time makes my brain hum. I can't stop thinking about pigeons. Someone has to break a record for pigeons. Someone has to.

And it will be me.

BACK TO SCHOOL

"You're back," Viva says as I walk into class. "And you don't smell."

Meanwhile, every kid is holding their nose and pretending I stink, but I know Grumpy Pigeon Man's concoction worked.

"Is Lonnie here yet?" I ask.

"No, what's up?"

There's still a lot of gagging going on, until Lonnie walks in and it stops. People respect Lonnie; they always have.

"Lonnie, I have to talk to you," I say.

Ms. Raffeli walks in then. She looks at me, smells the air, and smiles. "Welcome back, Teddy."

"Thanks."

"We have to talk," I whisper to Lonnie and Viva.

"Is everything okay?" Lonnie asks.

"I've got an idea."

"Teddy, Lonnie, Viva," Ms. Raffeli snaps. "We're waiting on you."

"I'll tell you at lunch."

THE BIG IDEA

I look around to be sure that in all the racket of the cafeteria no one is listening. "This is top secret."

"Okay," Viva says.

"No one except us can know," I say.

"We get it," Lonnie says.

I lean closer. "Most pigeons to land on a human."

"I assume you're talking about breaking a world record?" Lonnie asks.

"Yes."

"And you are the human?"

"Yes."

"And the pigeons are the fifty-seven ones owned by Grumpy Pigeon Man?"

"Yes."

"Most pigeons to land on a human," Viva repeats. "I like it."

"Me too," Lonnie says. "It's original. But how do you get them to land on you?"

"I've got it all figured out." Now that I've said it out loud I'm really excited. "Birdseed."

"Birdseed?" Lonnie asks.

"Remember those peanut butter birdseed pinecones The Destructor made at Christmas?" I ask Viva.

Lonnie says, "So you'll be the pinecone and spread peanut butter all over yourself and then put birdseed on top?"

"Exactly. The birds will land on me, eat the seed, and I'll have a world record."

"Have you told your parents?" Viva asks.

"No way."

"But your parents let you do everything," Viva says.

Lonnie shakes his head. "This feels like the

one thing you don't want to tell your parents."

"No one can know about this, not my parents, not my sisters, not Grumpy Pigeon Man, and definitely not The Destructor."

"Are you worried about Grumpy Pigeon Man?"

"Well, it won't hurt the birds at all. I figure, it'll take less than ten minutes, which is all the time they're allowed to eat anyway. After it's all done, we'll tell everyone. This time, I've done it properly. I filled out an application and have a number and everything. The record will be having fifty-seven pigeons on a human."

"What about proof?" Lonnie asks.

"I'll bring my camera and film the whole thing," Viva says.

"You'll be the only kid we know in *The Guinness Book of World Records*." Lonnie throws away his lunch. "So cool." He pauses. "What about the peanut butter? You'll need a lot."

"We've got loads of peanut butter in my basement. Mom buys it in bulk. And I'll use Grumpy Pigeon Man's birdseed."

"We need to pick a day," Viva says as the recess bell rings.

"What about next week?" Lonnie asks.

"That won't work," I say. "It's spring vacation.

My whole family will be around."

I can see Lonnie thinking about this. "Then how about this Saturday?"

"Saturdays are good," I say. And they are. My family is always in a million different places on Saturdays.

Viva nods. "That gives you five days to prepare."

"Okay. How about nine a.m.?" I say. "Grumpy Pigeon Man never comes out in the morning."

"This is going to be the best world record ever," Lonnie says. "Much better than the 4,010 pounds of stir-fry."

"So true," I say as we plow through the doors to the playground.

ALL FIXED

When I get home The Destructor is at the front door waiting. "Tent Boy! Tent Boy!" He drags me to the back door and points outside. There is my tent all set up and perfect.

"Thanks, Mom," I say.

"It was actually Jake's idea."

It's like this plan to set a world record has turned me inside out, and even though The Destructor is on my most wanted list I say, "Hey, Destructor, let's go check it out." His face lights up and he runs out the door. I grab the Oreos.

"Teddy!" Mom yells before we disappear. "Thanks. And don't forget Sharon's play is Saturday."

"Saturday? What time?"

"Noon," she says.

I frown.

"Do you have something to do?" she asks.

"Do we have to go?" I ask.

Mom smiles. "Yes."

I think about this. I'll be done by nine thirty at the latest. "Fine," I say.

"Close your eyes," The Destructor says, and pulls me into the tent.

"TA-DA!" he yells.

There's a bookshelf now and a beanbag chair. And all my books and Star Wars figures are in order from smallest to tallest.

"Mom washed everything in Mr. Marney's soap."

"Here's *The Guinness Book*. Smell it. It doesn't smell!" He grabs a cookie. "Someday you'll be in there," he says.

Before thinking I say, "Sooner than you think." It's part of my happy mood, but right away I regret it.

"Are you breaking a record? What record?" He jumps up all excited. Cookies spill everywhere.

"I've got to get the dustpan," I say and leap up. If there's one thing I've learned it's that there's no such thing as being too careful with skunks, or The Destructor. I am not taking any chances with either.

DAY 158
CLICK!

Grace steps on my foot on her way past. "Just to keep in practice," she says and walks away.

I've got bigger things to think about than Grace or my foot so this time I don't feel a thing.

PREPARATIONS
"Three days until I break a world record and three days until Sharon breaks our ears," I say. We're out with the pigeons.

"I can't believe my parents are making me go," Lonnie says.

Jar Jar Binks lands on my knee. "Are they just being nice to my family?"

"No. They say I'm in for a surprise. The only surprise would be if Yoda walked out in the middle." He holds up his hands like he's swinging a lightsaber. Then he sighs.

Viva holds out her hand to Admiral Ackbar. "My parents say they're only doing it to be supportive. They hate musicals."

Lonnie shakes his head. "They almost said I couldn't come over before the musical. I told them we had a project, which isn't exactly a lie. It is a project."

"How are the preparations going?" Viva asks.

"Good. I've got six jars hidden inside the pigeon food bin."

"I don't think that's enough," Viva says. "Lonnie, try to get more from your house. I will too. We only have almond butter, but it should work the same. What about eating extra grains so the pigeons like you more? Have you mapped out your plan? Do we put the peanut butter on in the aviary or outside the aviary and then you walk in? When do we apply the birdseed? And what are you going to wear?"

"Hey, Tent Boy! Hi, Lonnie! Hi, Viva!" The

Destructor waves frantically from across the fence. "Can I come over?"

"No!" I say.

"What are you doing?" he yells.

"Nothing."

"You should break a world record," he yells louder. "You know you could do it, Teddy."

"Go away, Destructor." I wait until he's moved away from the fence and is out of earshot. "Do you think he heard us?"

"No," Viva says. "Anyway what can he do?"

I shake my head. "Everything."

The Destructor zigzags across the yard like a mosquito. Strange but true, in *The Guinness Book of World Records* there is a record for most dangerous mosquito. That bug has caused 50 percent of all human deaths since the Stone Age (excluding wars and accidents).

The Destructor is possibly a close relative, and I've got to be very careful.

FOLLOWING VIVA'S ADVICE

Luckily, Viva thinks about things in this super weird way that helps you do something better.

So for the rest of the week I sneak four jars

of peanut butter out of the house every day. It's only because my family shops for two months at a time and keeps it in the basement that I'm able to do this and have no one notice—no one except for The Destructor, who was in his cat box one afternoon as I snuck past.

"What are you doing with all the peanut butter?"

"School project," I say. And keep moving. I can't remember what else Viva told me to do, but I'm sure it'll all work out.

THE DAY BEFORE THE BIG DAY

It's Friday, the day before the big day, the doozy of the day, when I break a world record. It's also Sharon's big day.

At breakfast Sharon is so excited she's about to explode. I feel the same way.

"Stop jumping on the sofa!" Mom shouts at me

from the kitchen. "What is up with you? You've got more beans than Sharon."

Mom is in hyper mode and is going over the schedule with all of us like we're in preschool. "Tonight is opening night."

"What's opening night?" The Destructor asks from the cat box, where he's eating his breakfast.

"The first night of the play," Mom explains.

"When are we going?" he asks.

"Tomorrow afternoon," Mom says.

"Why can't we go to the *opening*?" The Destructor says *opening* like it's a different language.

Sharon pipes up, "Because there is no way my family is ruining it. You're going to the matinee, which is filled with kids and grandparents, and you'll all blend in."

She really doesn't trust us, and I get it.

And then, out of nowhere The Destructor crawls out of the cat box, toast in his hand, and climbs onto a chair. I do a double take. He's actually eating at the table.

"Don't say a word," Mom whispers in my ear.

There are just three entries in *The Guinness Book of World Records* for rare things. One is a plant, one is a tree, and one is something called a "speech sound" (really), but I think maybe The Destructor could join them. Rarest appearance for eating at a table.

THE DAY

I wake up. I'm sweaty and hot. In the middle of the night I kicked off my blankets, but it didn't make a difference. The tent is stifling. I unzip it and go outside. It's an absurdly hot day.

There goes my plan to wear my old sweatshirt and pants. I'll find a T-shirt and shorts in my room.

In the house things are quiet. Dad and The Destructor are awake. The Destructor is sitting at the table again. I don't know what's happening to him.

"Where is everyone?" I ask.

"Grace's still asleep. Casey and Caitlin are out on their bikes practicing for trash hauling. Maggie's at soccer practice. Mom's taking Sharon to the school theater and staying to help out."

As I go upstairs to find clothes I review my plan:

5:30: Pretend to feed the pigeons. (We want them super hungry so they eat off me.)

9:00: Lonnie and Viva show up. (I've already

told Dad that we're doing a project and not to bother us.)

9:05: Lonnie and Viva apply the peanut butter and birdseed.

9:10: Break the world record.

9:15: Done.

"Can I feed the pigeons with you?" The Destructor asks.

"No." Like Sharon, I'm not taking any chances. "I'll take you tomorrow."

"Why don't you let him tag along?" Dad asks.

"School project." I feel lousy lying, but I have to. "Oh, and we need these." I grab two spatulas and slip out.

RECORD ATTEMPT 10: PEANUT BUTTER

Lonnie and Viva show up. I'm in the loft giving water to the birds, in case they're as hot as I am.

"Let's go," I say. I realize I'm nervous, but I can't decide if it's about breaking a world record or getting caught before I break a world record.

All the pigeons are in the loft and I close the door separating the two sections. I hand Lonnie and Viva the spatulas and the peanut butter jars that I fished out of the food bin.

They start to spread.

"Good thinking with the spatulas," Viva says.

"Hold still, Teddy," Lonnie says.

"Sorry, it tickles."

They smear peanut butter all over my arms, my hands, my back, and my front, on the top of my head and all over my legs and feet. Lonnie stops for a second and looks at me real serious.

"I didn't want to, but I've got to ask." He cringes. "What about your privates?"

Viva smothers a laugh. I ignore her. A world record breaker has to be able to stand up to more than a giggle. Take Monsieur Mangetout, famous for eating metal and glass. The guy ate a bicycle once! I don't care what anyone says, that has got to hurt. So I can handle a few giggles.

"No thanks," I say as if he asked if I wanted a soda.

Being covered in peanut butter probably feels gross at any time, but on a hot day it has to be the grossest. It oozes through my clothes, drips on my skin, and is way more oily than I like to think about.

"It's already nine thirty," Lonnie says.

"Shake the birdseed on me. Quick." I admit I'm nervous that Grumpy Pigeon Man will walk out. Every little noise startles me.

They sprinkle the seed all over me. I can't feel any of it because of the peanut butter.

"Done," Lonnie says. "It's nine forty-five."

"Right." Viva picks up her camera. "Lonnie, your job is to get all the pigeons on him."

"Ready?"

"Ready."

RECORD ATTEMPT 10: HUMAN BIRD FEEDER

The pigeons should be really hungry since I haven't fed them. But they're not acting like it. They're just hanging out doing their thing.

I stand there, waiting. They still don't move. "Should I do something?"

"Pretend you're a birdfeeder." Lonnie laughs.

"Ha, ha," I say.

"Don't worry," Viva says. "They'll come." After a few more seconds of the birds doing nothing, finally Paploo lands on my shoulder. His little feet grasp onto my shirt. His wings flap, then he starts to eat. Once he starts in, another pigeon flies over, then another, then another.

"I see about ten," Lonnie says.

"Only ten?" I say. "It feels like more."

"No, it's definitely ten."

"Chase some more pigeons onto him," Viva says.

Lonnie waves more over. They run away from him but get the hint and land. It is very ticklish having this many pigeons on me. They peck off the birdseed from my arms and back. "Maybe I should sit down so they can get my legs?"

"Good thinking," Lonnie says. I sit down, stretching my legs straight out in front of me.

Viva circles around. "I want to be sure I film all the pigeons."

Lonnie says, "It's hard to count them. They keep moving."

The tickling becomes more like scratches as the birds fight for space.

"Twenty!" Lonnie sounds excited.

"Sit up straight," Viva orders. "They won't all fit if you're hunched up."

"I can't help it," I say. A bird pecks food off my foot. My foot jerks and three birds flutter away.

"Don't scare the pigeons," Lonnie says.

"I don't mean to," I say. Clearly, I did not think through what fifty-seven birds landing on me would be like, because having twenty is a real challenge.

I can't stay sitting anymore. I slowly stand up. Now that they know there's birdseed on my legs they cling to me for dear life. They hook their feet into my shorts, and my legs, and don't fall off. It's painful.

"You've got thirty pigeons on you," Lonnie says. He sends more pigeons my way.

"As weird as this sounds," I say, "the pigeons poking actually hurts." I flinch as a bird gets me in the neck. "Does it really matter if I have all of them? I mean, thirty should get me into *The Guinness Book of World Records*, right?"

"I think you can stop when you want to," Lonnie says. "You'll break the record no matter what."

"No," Viva says. "You said fifty-seven in your application. You've got to do all fifty-seven."

It's true that we talked about this, but I forgot to find out the rule.

"I count forty now," Lonnie says.

I try to think about Elaine Davidson, the most pierced woman in the world, with 4,225 piercings, and what *that* would feel like, but a pigeon pecking my head distracts me.

For some reason, now that one bird figured out my head was made of birdseed, they all have.

This is not good.

"Stop hopping," Lonnie says. "You're scaring them."

"I didn't know I was hopping." It seems my body has separated from my brain and decided to do whatever it wants. It jerks and jumps at each peck. "Hurry, Lonnie. I can't do this much longer."

"Of course you can," Viva says. "Only seventeen more."

I shudder as two more land on the back of my neck. My arms begin to flail. I'm also losing my balance as the birds flap, pulling me in different directions.

"Quick, Lonnie! Get the rest of them. He's weakening."

Lonnie says, "I think we should stop." More birds land on me.

"He doesn't want to stop. Do you want to stop?"

"I don't know," I say from under the pile of pigeons.

"Only nine more!" Viva says. "Don't give up now!"

My body and brain have a different idea from Viva. I shake, jitter, and jump. I squirm, squiggle, and leap while the birds peck, scratch, and eat me. Clearly, they're on Viva's side.

It's hard to see anything with all the feathers flapping in my face, but between their beating wings I see Lonnie and Viva trying to scoot the last birds toward me. Viva still films as she chases them over.

Suddenly, the birds are not happy. They push each other out of the way. They cling to my body fighting for the last seed. They poke at my feet, my arms, my head, and my legs. It's too much. I wave my arms, trying to get them off. I holler, hoping to scare them. They pull me this way and that until I finally fall over, screaming as I hit the ground.

And then a voice cuts through: "I'LL SAVE YOU!" And The Destructor runs in. His arms spin like a windmill, and he's yelling at the top of his lungs.

RECORD ATTEMPT 10: DESTRUCTION

The Destructor keeps shouting and flailing his arms. He crashes into Viva. The camera jerks out of her hand but she catches it. Pigeons flap in every direction, terrified by The Destructor. A bird flies into Viva's hair and gets all twisted up. She struggles to untangle it. The Destructor pushes Lonnie out of the loft and runs back to Viva. He pulls the pigeon free, then shoves her toward the door. She trips.

"The camera!" she yells as she's forced outside.

The camera flips over and over and dives straight into the birdbath, clanging on the metal before it sinks to the bottom.

I reach into the birdbath and grab the sopping camera as The Destructor pulls me to my feet, waving his hands all around. The birds fly off me and he pulls me out and into the open air, slamming the door behind him.

"Teddy." Viva frowns. "The camera. The birdbath."

I hold it up. "It's got to work," I say. "Without that there's no proof."

Lonnie steps forward. The camera drips in his hand. He presses buttons, dries it on his clothes, presses more buttons, then shakes his head. "It's not working."

The Destructor stays close to me. He smiles.

"Are you okay?"

"Am I okay?" I repeat. "Don't you see what happened?! My world record! I might have had a chance, but without the camera, there's no way. I'll never break the record. You ruined it!" I'd like to jump on him. To pounce on him. To rip him into tiny pieces. "I wish you'd never been born!"

His smile melts. He stares at me, then he turns and runs away, and I don't care because it's his fault. Everything is his fault.

TENT BOY? IS THAT YOU?

Grumpy Pigeon Man comes out of his house. "Tent Boy?" he asks. "Is that you?"

I don't know what I look like but clearly I don't look like me. I push past him and run to my house. I don't have any words. I run. I run like Maggie runs. My feet pound up to our house, up the stairs, through the hall past Dad, past Casey and Caitlin, who are back from their bike adventures, past Maggie, who's stretching, past Grace, who's got a paintbrush in her hand. I dash to the upstairs bathroom and slam and lock the door like Sharon does.

I turn on the shower and climb into it, clothes

and all. What was I thinking trying to break a world record? Trying to do one thing that The Destructor couldn't destroy. What an idiot.

"Teddy?" Dad knocks. "Teddy? Let me in."

"Go away," I shout through the water. "Go away."

"Teddy, what's going on? Where's Jake?"

"I don't know. You're the dad, you find him."

"Teddy, come out of the bathroom right now."

"No." I can't believe I'm saying this. Of course I should come out, but I can't.

I turn off the shower and listen as he calls for Jake. I hear Maggie, Casey, Caitlin, even Grace calling for Jake. And then I hear the front door slam.

I turn the shower back on and scrub every bit of peanut butter and birdseed off.

CHER AMI RETURNS

"Tent Boy, it's me." I sit up. I wipe drool off my cheek. I must have fallen asleep. I look at my clock. It's three. I missed Sharon's show.

I unzip the tent partway. Grumpy Pigeon Man leans down. "We still can't find him," he says.

"So what?"

"He's been missing since this morning."

"He'll turn up," I say.

"Come out, Tent Boy. You can't hide in there forever."

"Are you sure?" I ask.

"Then let me in."

I open the tent. Grumpy Pigeon Man climbs in and sits down. He's tall. With him in here, there isn't much room.

"You know he tried to save you."

"Nobody asked him to."

"That's true, but he did what he thought was right. Now you have to do what's right."

I open my mouth to argue, but then close it.

"Tent Boy, all I'm going to say is: Cher Ami."

I'm quiet for a while, then say, "It's a point, Mr. Marney. I just don't know if it's a good one."

"Don't you get it, Tent Boy? You are Jake's Cher Ami, his hero. Jake was scared for you. Don't hold that against him. Whatever you think about him, change it."

The first time I opened *The Guinness Book of World Records*, it just clicked in my brain. Right away, I got it. And suddenly just like that, I get it.

Grumpy Pigeon Man's words click.

I think about all the world records, and all the people setting records. The book is about change. That's why every year they have to bring out a new version. I mean, even the world record for longest hot dog changes almost every year. Strange but true, somehow someone makes a longer hot dog. Will it ever stop? Only if people stop believing in change.

"Okay," I say. "I'll find him, Mr. Marney."

"Good. And don't call me Mr. Marney. Grumpy Pigeon Man will do."

How did he know I called him that?

"You thought I was asleep in the hospital," he says.

LIKE A PIGEON

I know my family really, really well, so I know all the places they have already looked. I know that they already looked all over the house, in his room, in the basement, in the backyard, in all the nooks and crannies he could fit inside. But I know The Destructor like no one else. My homing instincts kick in. It's like The Destructor is my home and I am Cher Ami. He's easy to find.

I walk straight into the aviary. And even though all that crazy stuff happened, I'm not scared of the pigeons. They're all calm now again. I lean down so I can look inside the nesting box closest to the ground and off in the farthest corner. There's Jake. Curled up and fast asleep, snoring, and of course covered in pigeon poo.

I kneel down. "Wake up, Jake," I say, shaking him a little. His eyes open.

"I'm not coming out."

"You really need a bath."

"I'm staying here."

"You can't stay here."

"Why not?"

"Mom and Dad would miss you."

"Who cares," he says. "You never miss me."

I think about this and deep down, deep, deep, deep down I do miss him. "What if I move back into the house?" I ask.

"Would you move back into our room?"

"Would you leave my things alone?"

"Yeah," he says. And even though I don't believe him, I know I'll give him a chance to change.

"Okay, it's a deal." Jake crawls out and wraps his arms around me.

"Oh great," I say. "Now I need another shower."

FAILURE

"Get off, Mom!" I say, but she doesn't. She's hugging and kissing me. "You found him. You found Jake."

Dad comes up and hugs me too. "We've got to get going if we're going to make it to the performance." And we all pile into the van for Sharon's show, even Grumpy Pigeon Man. I try to smile but I don't really feel like it.

Grace punches me. "You were *almost* my hero when I thought we'd get out of going to this dumb show. Who knew Mom would manage to trade our tickets for tonight?"

"Grace," Mom warns.

The theater is packed. Lonnie waves and Viva looks over and smiles. I'm glad to see that Viva's hair looks normal. Considering what she went through, I wasn't sure. But I have to admit, seeing them makes my stomach drop. Luckily, it's too crowded for them to come close.

It's not just that Viva's camera broke and I'll be working for Grumpy Pigeon Man forever to pay for a new one. It's because I failed.

Again.

WEIRDNESS EXPLAINED

The lights flicker and then they go off completely. We all sit down quickly and the music starts. We're about two minutes into it when Lonnie's brother, Jerome, steps onto the stage.

He's in the play! This explains why Lonnie had to come.

Then Sharon walks out. It's like she isn't my sister. It's like she's totally somebody else.

It doesn't take too long to figure out that in the play they're supposed to fall in love. Maybe this is why Jerome's been so nice.

But it's at the end of the play when the craziest thing happens. All the actors come out to bow, and they're all holding hands, including Sharon and Jerome, but after the bow everyone else lets go except for them, and then, I hate to say this, they kiss.

Luckily this kiss does not last as long as the longest kiss in *The Guinness Book of World Records*: 58 hours 35 minutes 58 seconds, which is revolting for so many reasons, but it lasts long enough for all of us to know that they are in love. Now I know why Jerome's been so weird. Viva was right. It isn't alien brain invasion. It's a girlfriend, and it's my sister.

And then the lights come on. Lonnie and Viva make their way to me and we head out of the theater and into the hallway.

"Can you believe that?" Lonnie says.

"Sharon and Jerome are together," I say. "Ewww."

"Ewww," Lonnie agrees.

"Totally ewww," Viva says.

"I'm so sorry about today," I say.

"What for?" Viva asks. "It was the best. My parents would never let me pull a stunt like that."

Lonnie smiles. "Viva and I have spring vacation all figured out."

Viva says, "Starting Monday we begin to plan another record."

Lonnie nods. "But this time something about Star Wars."

I shrug. I'm not sure I'm up for any more world record disappointment.

SLEEPOVER

It's my last night in the tent. Jake and I are side by side in our sleeping bags. After today I knew I had to include The Destructor.

"Let's stay up all night," he says.

"I don't think I can."

"OOOOOOKLAHOOOOOOMAAAAA!"

Jake sings. He's been singing it ever since Sharon's play. "Can I live out here with you?" Jake yawns.

"We already decided. I'm moving back inside."

"We should live out here," he says, yawning again. "It's nice and quiet. There are too many people in our house."

"Grumpy Pigeon Man said only pigeons are crazy enough to like living with so many. He was wrong." The Destructor interrupts me with a remarkably loud snore. He's asleep but I keep talking. "Pigeons like being together and they always go home. I guess if that's crazy then I'm as crazy as a pigeon."

The Destructor pats my hand. "You are crazy," he says, rolling over and letting out another honking big snore.

NEWS

When we wake up we go inside for breakfast. Mom is setting out forks, knives, and plates. Dad is flipping pancakes. Sharon, Caitlin and Casey, and Maggie are in the living room.

"Sit here," Grace says. "And don't move."

"Uh," I say, looking down just to be sure there aren't tacks on the chair. She runs out of the room.

The Destructor follows. The doorbell rings.

"I'll get it," Caitlin shouts.

"What's going on?" I ask.

"Nothing," Mom says. "Just a few people are coming over."

Lonnie, Jerome, and their parents walk in. Lonnie looks really serious and I wonder if we're in trouble. Sharon drags Jerome into the other room. She looks at me and says, "Stay."

The doorbell rings a minute later. "I'll get it," Casey yells.

Viva and her parents walk in. They look really, really serious and my heart starts pounding because it's got to be trouble.

There's a knock at the back door and Grumpy Pigeon Man shows up. He nods and takes a seat. Now I know we're all going to be punished for yesterday. I mean, it had to happen. We broke about a million rules. Actually, I broke about a million rules.

The doorbell rings again. Caitlin and Casey holler, "We got it!"

When Ms. Raffeli walks in, I nearly fall off my chair. Lonnie and Viva walk out of the kitchen, which makes me even more nervous. Now I'm alone with all the grown-ups. I try to inch my way out of the room, but Mom says, "Don't move! We need to talk."

Dad frowns and says, "We've got some news."

Now I'm sure I'm in trouble.

MORE ABOUT THE NEWS

"News?" My throat burns. "I'm really sorry," I blurt out. "I promise I won't try to break any more world records. And don't be mad at Lonnie and Viva." I look at their parents. "It was all my fault."

Just then Sharon, Caitlin and Casey, Maggie, Grace, The Destructor, Lonnie, and Viva walk into the kitchen holding a tube of paper all rolled up.

I'm so confused I can't figure out what is going on.

"Teddy!" The Destructor jumps up and down. "You did it! You broke a world record!"

"I didn't do anything."

"Actually, Tent Boy," Grace says, stepping to the side. "You did." At that second they unroll the tube.

In big painted letters, it says: TEDDY MARS, WORLD RECORD BREAKER!

Mom runs over and hugs me. Dad swoops down, too.

Sharon says, "We sent in an application for you."

Caitlin and Casey say, "Your record is: the longest time sleeping in a tent for anyone under the age of twelve!"

Maggie says, "You slept there for 162 days."

Lonnie gives me a high five.

Mom says, "The World Record people got in touch yesterday, but with everything going on we decided to wait until today to tell you."

The Destructor pats me on my back. "I knew you'd break a record."

Strange but true, my family did this for me. I look around and see Ms. Raffeli. She gives me a thumbs-up. Lonnie and his folks are beaming. Grumpy Pigeon Man is grinning from ear to ear just like the rest of my huge, crazy family, and even though our families couldn't be more different, Viva's parents are smiling too.

"It was all thanks to Grace," Dad adds. "If she hadn't taken pictures the whole time it wouldn't have happened."

"Thanks, Grace," I say.

"Don't think I did this for you," she says. "It was just a way to make the whole world know."

"To make the whole world know what?" I ask.

"That you are a nut-o named Tent Boy. Now my job is complete." She smiles and steps on my foot.

Strange but true, this time it didn't hurt so much, and stranger but truer, this time I don't mind being called Tent Boy.

MY BROTHER, JAKE, PART 2

"We'll be here first thing tomorrow morning," Lonnie yells as his family drives away.

"This is going to be the best vacation ever," Viva says. Her mom pulls her out the front door.

And she's right because even though I did break a record, we all know there are more records to break. And we have nothing to do for a whole week except think them up!

Ms. Raffeli hugs me. "I don't want any world record business when we come back to school." I know she means it because her eyebrows go up.

Grumpy Pigeon Man shakes my hand. "And

don't forget about the pigeons."

"I'm going right now," I say and turn to The Destructor. "Want to come?"

He runs right out the door.

I get water while he stays in the aviary watching the birds. I have to admit, everything seems so peaceful.

Then I hear him. "I'm Pigeon Boy! I'm Pigeon Boy!"

I walk in and drop the bucket. Unbelievably, he's *covered* in feathers.

"Don't worry, Teddy. They're from the floor. I didn't pluck a pigeon. And the poo makes them stick. Look!" He picks up a feather, scrapes it on some poo, and then sticks it to his clothes. He's right. Bird poo is sticky. "You can call me Pigeon Boy. I save pigeons from evildoers!" He puts his hands on his hips and looks even more like a bird.

Poor Destructor, he will never be normal. I guess it just doesn't run in our family. But maybe normal is not all it's cracked up to be.

If everyone were normal they wouldn't try to break world records. And if everyone were normal they wouldn't keep pigeons, or dream of being Jedi warriors, or help a friend break a world record.

If everyone were normal they wouldn't collect trash on bikes, or save a brother from a flock of pigeons, or sing, or run, or take pictures, or even have seven kids and let those kids be who they are and not fuss about every little thing they do.

If everyone were normal they wouldn't live in a tent for 162 days, and if everyone were normal The Destructor would definitely not be covered in pigeon poo and feathers right now calling himself Pigeon Boy.

But he is.

And strange but true, I'm fine with that.

ACKNOWLEDGMENTS

1. Sean Greene—my best friend, favorite artist, and collaborator.
2. My parents—who never let me quit.
3. My sister—who always trusted I could do this.
4. Tina Wexler—my enthusiastic, brilliant, and hilarious agent!
5. Katherine Tegen—for believing in Teddy and appreciating farts.
6. Maria Barbo—you are a present in Teddy's life but even more so in mine!
7. Molly O'Neill—your penciled hearts quieted my first fears.
8. The team at Katherine Tegen Books and HarperCollins—Amy Ryan, Erin Fitzsimmons, Bethany Reis, Mark Rifkin, Lauren Flower, Ro Romanello, Jean McGinley, Alpha Wong, Sarah Oughton, Colleen Prendergast, Sheala Howley—for thoughtfully

and elegantly working your magic.

9. Trevor Spencer—your pictures crack me up!

10. Hamline University MFAC faculty and students—for teaching, challenging, and encouraging.

11. Cheryl Bardoe, Yolanda Hare, Jill Davis, Elizabeth Schoenberg, and Madelyn Rosenberg—my writing friends who became friends.

12. Judy Blume, Louis Sachar, and Barbara Park—your writing amazes me.

13. Stephen Roxburgh and Carolyn Coman—two fabulous visionaries.

14. Highlights Foundation—you gave me time with this book.

15. Jackson Street School students and teachers and the Pedal People of Northampton, and my next-door neighbors and their pigeons—educating all of us on how to live right.

16. And last but not least *The Guinness Book of World Records* and all the people who break records! Without you, there would be no book!